The Peaceful

Storm

The Peaceful Storm

Charles F. Robertson

With Cliff Dudley

New Leaf ❧ Press

P.O. BOX 311, GREEN FOREST, AR 72638

FIRST EDITION, 1985

Cover Art: Karen O'Dell

Typesetting by SPACE
(Sharp Printing & Computer Enterprise)
Berryville, AR 72616

Library of Congress Number: 85-73480
ISBN Number: 0-89221-135-0

CONTENTS

Dedication

To my faithful, loving wife, Gunda; and

To my precious children, Charles, Brittarose, Darlene and Kay; and

To the entire staff of the Elna M. Smith Foundation.

Chapter One

The Printer's Son

"Chancy, Honey, it's time and we had better hurry!" Britta tenderly commanded her husband.

"Stay calm, don't panic, everything is going to be all right. Where is your suitcase? I'll get the buggy. Don't get excited, it will only take a minute or two and I will be right back. Oh, I have got to put my shoes on first," was Chancy's "calm" reply.

"Of course, Honey, everything is all right. I will walk to the buggy with you, so you won't go off and leave me here," Britta chuckled.

As the two of them stepped out of the doorway, the day which was May 25, 1915, seemed otherwise calm and peaceful. The awesome smokestacks of the steel mill loomed high above the skyline. Today, this very special day, they seemed to be belching forth more than the usual amount of their orange colored demon-like smoke. The entire valley was blanketed with the eerie cloud from the mill's blast furnaces. The beauty of the Ohio River and the splendor of the mountains were all but lost to the fury of the creeping death. However, both Chancy and

Britta knew that it was "that smoke" that kept the city of Follansbee, West Virginia alive.

They got into the buggy and raced to the hospital. In moments the buggy came to a screeching halt at the entrance to the hospital and from that moment Chancy lost control of the situation and the nurses took over.

"Mr. Robertson," one said, "Please be seated in the waiting room and the doctor will notify you when the baby arrives." Chancy was pacing back and forth across the room when he looked up and saw his sister-in-law, Goldie Farrell. "Goldie," he asked. "What's taking so long?"

"Just be patient, CB, these things sometimes can take a long time," was her confident reply.

At that he continued to pace, pray, wait, pace, pray, wait some more.

"God, let everything be all right with Britta and the baby, please!" Chancy prayed.

After what seemed to be almost an eternity, Chancy looked up and saw the doctor coming down the hall with a big smile on his face.

The doctor spoke, "Chancy, it is a fine eleven-pound boy. Both Britta and your son are doing fine. By the way, what are you going to name him?"

"Charles Franklin," was my father's reply.

Thus my life began. . .

My father was one of Follansbee's businessmen, as he owned the town newspaper. He had worked hard after he left the Pittsburgh Sun Telegraph where he was well respected as one of the finest newsmen on their payroll. His paper started out as a weekly and then because of its success, my father was able to increase the publication to a bi-weekly. He planned to make it into a daily but time wasn't with him.

Father was a man of real conviction and was a practicing Christian and attended a large Presbyterian church. Every night after dinner my father would bring out his Bible, and the family would gather around him as he read the Word. We would always close our family

My parents, Chancy and Britta Robertson

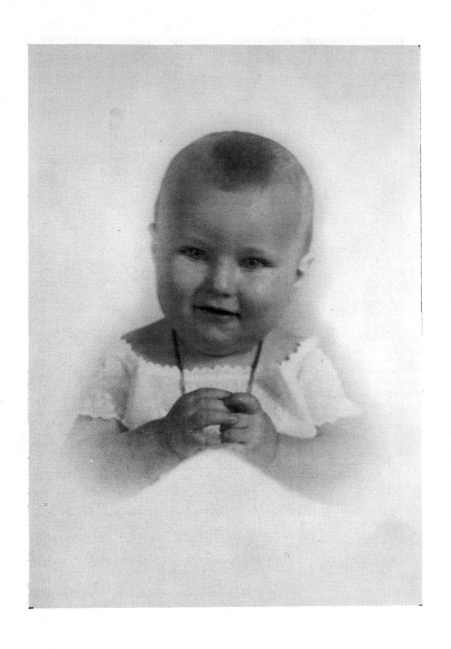

Charles Franklin Robertson

Bert and baby me

Dad's newspaper shop

Charles age 9

time with prayer. It was a rare exception when this wasn't done. That would be on the nights he would have to stay to make sure the paper would be ready for the next day's edition.

My father was a layman preacher and would speak wherever he was called upon. Even as a child he was very ecumenical because he loved to sing and would sing in the Presbyterian choir and then rush over to the Catholic church to sing in their choir. So during his childhood he got a well rounded education in doctrine. My mother was a very wonderful and compassionate woman. She kept an excellent home and was a fabulous cook. She worked right alongside of my father at the newspaper. She set the type for the newspaper. One day while changing the magazine on the typesetter, her long hair got caught in the cogs. Fortunately it was long enough that by the time it got down to her scalp, it clogged the machine, stopping it. In that day it was a real honor and considered very spiritual and fitting for a woman to have long hair. I am certain my mother was pleased that day that she had followed the Bible to the letter of the law.

Our home was typical of the homes of that period — there being a large living room and sitting room, three bedrooms and a kitchen and dining room. All the rooms were equipped with gas lamps as electricity at that time was still relatively scarce. Most all of our family talking and gathering centered around the sitting room as that's where the large pot-bellied stove was situated. What a wonderful privilege it was to come in out of the cold winter and gather around that stove for warmth and sing hymns.

Our home was located on the main street of town. The steel mill was between us and the Ohio River. Almost all of the streets in the town were either up or down. We lived in a very mountainous and hilly area. Bicycle riding was quite a trick for a five year old, especially when the bike had no brakes. More times than one trying to stop the bike downhill, I would hit a rock or a rut and over I

I would go skinning a knee, arm or what-have-you, but most of the time it was my pride that hurt the most. Often-times in the spring the Ohio River would go on a rampage and come out of its banks flooding the entire downtown section; however, it never reached our home while we lived there.

We lived a very simple and uncomplicated life and our food wasn't fancy but good and nourishing. I suppose we tended more towards meat, potatoes and gravy rather than pastries and desserts. One of the special things that father would serve when we had guests was fried oysters from the delicatessen down the street. Or he would send me to the ice cream store for a hand packed container of ice cream and invariably by the time I got home it seemed like they had only given me a pint.

My brother Bert had a full time job taking care of me and did a very good job. I remember one time when I had become quite ill and could not walk. Something was wrong with the circulation in my legs and therefore, for a time, I lost the use of them. They suspected I had rheumatic fever. It lasted for two years and eventually I outgrew the problem. My brother, or whatever kid he could con in the neighborhood, would haul me around, up and down the streets in my red wagon. I remember well the day we were going down the alley by my dad's newspaper when a man came along and said to the children, "Which of you is Charles Robertson?" They all pointed to me sitting in the red wagon and, much to my surprise and their surprise, the man grabbed me up off the blanket and started running full steam ahead down the alley. I didn't know what the word kidnap meant, but the boys were screaming and yelling, "He's kidnapping Charles, he's kidnapping Charles!" The boys started screaming, "Daddy, daddy, Mr. Robertson, Mr. Robertson, help, help, help!" Suddenly father loomed out of the door of the print shop and at a glance saw the situation and pursued us full steam ahead. The man who had me in his arms realized he was running a losing race and dropped me to save his own neck. My father was so

14

concerned about me that he stopped, and the man just kept running. To this day we never knew why he wanted to kidnap the son of Chancy Robertson. Oh, there was speculation all right. My father's editorials on the front page of the newspaper were very caustic to the illegal liquor dealers and the stills that were being run in the town. He painted liquor as a very ugly and vile thing. The paper never accepted any tobacco or liquor advertising. Also my father wasn't afraid to name names and fight for what was right in our town government; therefore, I know he had many secret enemies even though he was so highly respected by the townspeople.

My father's editorials prompted many police raids on various illegal industries that were being conducted in the town. There was a very strange phenomenon that took place after one such raid, because practically everyone that was involved in it from my father down, took on a strange case of pneumonia and soon thereafter died. This was bitter agony for me a young boy of seven to have lost his father. It was hard for me to comprehend, why?

My father had planned to move to California to finish studying and get his law degree. So after his death my mother started talking about moving her family to California to fulfill my father's wishes. After the kidnapping attempt, my mother was very protective of my brother and me. We had no more experiences of that nature. School was very interesting in those days as the teachers had absolute authority. My first grade school teacher's name was Miss Snodgrass. She was an absolute authoritarian. I can remember well the day when one of the students came in, she called him up to the front of the class and said, "All right Timmy, I have told you time and time again if you didn't scrub your neck, I would do it for you in front of the class." At that word she got the wash cloth, soaked it down and started scrubbing his neck obviously humiliating him in front of all the students. The boy's sister saw that, got up from her desk and ran out of the school to get her

15

mother. It wasn't long until the mother was back. She was mad and made quite a stir. I can still hear her shouts, "How dare you scrub my son's neck in front of the students? Don't you ever do that again!" Miss Snodgrass looked at the mother square in the eye and said to her, "Listen! You just hush and get out of this classroom before I scrub your neck." At that the mother walked out of the room defeated. The teacher had stood her ground. At that moment we all knew we had better mind because we knew who was boss! It was very obvious in our class of fifty that Miss Snodgrass was in total control of the entire operation. I probably got away with more things in the classroom than anyone else, even with occasionally being able to lay my head on the desk and take a nap. I don't know why she was so kind to me.

When I was five years old, the minister had Homer Rodeheaver, the great song writer and singer, come to the Presbyterian Church where we attended. After Mr. Rodeheaver sang and spoke he asked, "Those that want to dedicate their life to missionary work please come forward." I was impressed to say that I wanted to be a medical missionary. My mother's youngest brother was a surgeon and the head of the Mercy Hospital in Philadelphia. I guess that had some influence on me. I can remember distinctly how I was so impressed that that was what I should dedicate my life to.

Mother made preparations for us to leave West Virginia and move to California. My father had forgotten to change his insurance policy over to my mother's name when they married. Therefore, my mother was not the recipient of any insurance money. It was only the money that she received from the business and some of our furniture, etc., that enabled us to move to California. Many of our possessions were stored and left with "friends" that would ship them to us at a later date. We never again, however, saw any of it.

My mother was quite shocked over the insurance, but in reality my grandmother had to be cared for some way. I suppose this was as efficient as any way there was. Her husband had been in the Civil War and was quite mutilated from it and had already passed away in a military hospital.

We moved to the desert area of Southern California. I was quite amazed when we left our smoke-laden town to discover that the sun shone brightly and the stars and the moon glistened at night. I had certainly become used to constant pollution. We stayed at my Aunt's house in the city of Long Beach. We were there for about a year and then we moved to the city of Compton. It was literally like moving onto the sand of a beach. Everywhere you looked there was sand. But we soon learned that sand responds to water. Our grass and vegetables grew quickly. Much to my dismay (and my legs') school was three miles away, and there were no busses. That meant my brother and I had a six mile walk every day. We certainly didn't have to worry about jogging for exercise.

Mother got a job at a newspaper and worked, it seemed to us, almost night and day. My brother and I had to care for ourselves most of the time. I got a job selling newspapers. My salary was a penny a piece for every one I sold. So if I was fortunate to sell twenty-five papers, I made 25 cents for my day's labor. Walking to and from school we made quite a few new friends. My life soon became rather routine and uneventful.

There were no Presbyterian churches in the area. So we attended a brand new Christian Church which had just been founded. The pastor there was a man by the name of Rev. Arrent. What a wonderful man of God he was, for it was there under his ministry at the age of eleven I accepted Jesus as my Lord and Saviour.

Most everyone thinks of California as the warm hot climate where it never gets cold. I soon discovered that February can be very cold and chilly in the deserts of California. It was on such a cold February Sunday that I was going to follow the Lord in baptism. The baptistry had no heating element so it was a very cold baptism.

My brother Bert had decided to go to Bible School in Eugene, Oregon. My mother, not wanting him to be there alone, decided we should move there also. I was now in high school, but we all agreed and found ourselves Oregon bound. We stayed there only a year and then returned to live in Los Angeles.

My mother's sister Goldie had been very ill and nothing seemed to help her. She had heard of some of the miraculous and marvelous things that God was doing at a relatively new church that was pastored by a woman with the name of Aimee Semple McPherson. The name of the church was Angelus Temple. My Aunt Goldie, while attending there, went forward to be prayed for and was totally healed. Needless to say when we moved back into the Los Angeles area we received strong persuasion to attend this miracle lighthouse church. Nobody ever had to ask us to go there twice after experiencing the first meeting. We knew that the Power of God and the presence of the Holy Spirit were indeed at Angelus Temple. As a result, we made it our church home and became very involved in the activities of the church.

I thought Angelus Temple was the greatest and one of the largest places in all the world. It had a seating capacity of 5,200. People would gather early for services, lining up out on the streets so they would have a chance to get into the service. The whole atmosphere was very vibrant and enthusiastic. People were hungry for the Lord and God was blessing. That would have been in 1931 in the midst of the Great Depression.

One thing I enjoyed about Angelus Temple was helping in the soup lines. Men would come in to eat in their $300.00 suits and yet at that time be penniless. Their hands indicated that they had never done an hour's work outside of pushing a pencil. Many times during the week we would load large pots of soup on a truck and take the food to the people on the streets. Bowls, spoons and all. Of course there was no plastic so we had to return to the church and wash dishes. We were able to not only feed the people but we would see them come to the Lord as a result. The church had a commissary which was very busy all the time. Because even in those days welfare took so long helping those in need. We would pack boxes and baskets of perishables and various food stuffs and take them to the different homes where the people needed it now! This would tide them over until they could get other help. We also had complete layettes prepared for those who had just had a baby. The commissary was probably the center of activity of the church at that time, because so many were in need. Those who had a little bit were willing to share with those who had none. There wasn't much money in those days. From an audience of 5,000 people there would often only be $50.00 in the offering plates. There was no way for anybody to get rich off of the offerings in those days.

My life was so exciting and full of activity at Angelus Temple. When I was near eighteen, I was assigned to work in the dressing and makeup room. Sister McPherson most of the time preached illustrated sermons. That is, she preached as players would act out her sermon. Most of her spoken sermons on Sunday morning were very short in the range of twenty minutes. Her philosophy was that if you can't say it in twenty minutes, you just couldn't say it. Her Sunday night sermons were mostly illustrated. She would merely give us a skeleton outline of the scene and then verbally told us what she wanted. Her preaching was so dynamic that you could just flow in and sense what she was going to ask the players to do. For example, if she was preaching on Samson or David and Goliath, there would not only be actors but we would have elaborate back drops and gorgeous scenes. There would even be pillars that Samson could push down. She really put on a play while she preached. And those who saw them remembered them.

She wrote several oratorios. These were full fledged productions, oftentimes two hours in length. Her sermons made the gospel come alive to such an extent that there were literally hundreds at every service that would come to the alter for salvation, healing or whatever their needs might be. The altar workers were so well organized that they moved in and helped to meet these needs. They could answer almost any question that could be asked of them. They had the faith to pray for anything. They would stay believing God until results were evident. Then there were the prayer lines. People would come by the hundreds for Sister McPherson to pray for them. She would stay until the last soul had been prayed for. Many times almost having to be carried off because she was totally exhausted. Miracles followed her ministry. People were healed by the thousands. As a matter of fact, there was a room on the second floor of the church where you could go and see all the crutches, braces and paraphernalia people would throw away as God would touch their bodies. No one was ever turned away that was in need.

Angelus Temple came along in the middle of the great Pentecostal movement in the early 1900's. The temple which was circular in design was built around 1925. They referred to it as having three balconies. But actually it was two balconies and a half. The acoustics were outstanding. One could stand on the platform and speak in a mere whisper and their voice could be heard as far away as the third balcony. It was built before the day of the P.A. systems so therefore acoustics had to be the very best.

My memory takes me back to when Dr. Walkem came to the temple to give a piano recital. He had had many requests to play *"Harp Of A Thousand Strings."* "People," he said, "I don't think I should play this particular song here at the Temple." At that the congregation overwhelmingly applauded requesting him to play it. He looked up to the third balcony and remarked, "There is a light up there in the balcony and if there is anyone sitting under it I want you to cover your head or move. I am certain before this piece is over the light bulb will blow up." He began playing and sure enough, the light bulb exploded from the vibrations sent forth by the master's touch on the piano.

My life was changed and inspired by the years that I attended Angelus Temple. It was there that I received the call to go to Bible college. I knew that I needed more of the Word and had an overwhelming compulsion to attend L.I.F.E. Bible College which was the college run by the International Church of the Foursquare Gospel. Little did I know at the time God was dealing with a young girl by the name of Gunda Simonsen. She had attended a little store-front church and it was there that she gave her heart to the Lord Jesus. Soon after her conversion, her father, who was a very well known contractor having worked for Warner Brothers Studios and was one of the contractors that built the Hollywood Bowl, told her that she must stop going to that radical store-front church. He insisted that if she wanted to waste her life going to such a church she could leave the home. At that his daughter left, got a room with a girl friend and decided that she, too, was called to attend L.I.F.E. Bible College.

In those days the Foursquare organization was in its infancy. They had many store-front churches springing up all over the Los Angeles area. It was such a church that Gunda was attending. Some had meager beginnings, but later became large and outstanding.

The Bible College originally was designed to give layman training for there were so many, in those days, who wanted to go into the ministry to spread the gospel. Upon graduation, you were given a license to preach. Part of our training at Bible college would be actual training in the field, preaching, singing where ever God would provide a means. Some of us students decided that we would form a group and call it "Joy Bringers." We would travel around to different churches in the Long Beach pike area where we held outdoor services on the pier. We had a band somewhat like a Salvation Army band. I played the trombone. There was a girl who joined our group who led the singing and testified. The more we ministered for the Lord the more I seemed to notice her.

Soon after graduation from Bible school I went up north with two other boys to Mankato, Minnesota to establish a church there. It wasn't long until we had reasonable success. We moved into an old garage, did some painting and fixing up and converted it into a chapel. Before long we had quite a few people there worshipping Jesus.

Although I'd been exposed to the baptism of the Holy Spirit for quite some time and believed in it, I had never experienced it. I never could understand why until one day I got desperate. It wasn't easy as we were in the middle of the Depression. We were having quite a difficult time getting enough money in offerings to make ends meet. In a Monday night prayer meeting I really got down to business with the Lord. We were praying for others that had needs whether salvation, the baptism of the Holy Spirit or physical needs. I really got in earnest and I received the baptism much to my surprise because I wasn't at that particular time seeking. I was praying for and thinking of others. But the Lord filled me at that time. It was a cold winter night. We were in an old hosiery factory and it was difficult to generate enough heat to keep warm. However, we all got warm that night by the power of God. From then on, the ministry took on entirely different dimemsion and we saw the hand of God move in many, many wonderful ways.

After the church was established, I left my friend and went to the St. Peter area to begin a church there which was only about thirty miles away. The two of us were still working very close together even though we were now in different towns. We relied and leaned upon each other very much. I had rented the ballroom in the hotel as my meeting place. We were having a full house every time we opened the door.

The Presbyterian church was the leading church in town and the Christian church was second. When we started having services, people began flocking in and the local churches decided they had to do something. Scores were coming to our new church and they still had their same numbers, not growing. As a result, the town had a revival. Several miles away was a town by the name of Ottowa. We had thirty young people coming from Ottowa over to St. Peter for services. They were all under twenty-five and they would walk over. The congregation would, however, take them home to Ottowa after the services were over. I didn't realize what a gold mine I had in those young people. That was the fire that was sparking the whole community.

St. Peter was the site for the mental hospital of Minnesota. They had a lot of good people behind the fences. We were called to the institution by the superintendent who said that he was having difficulty with a man and his wife. The wife had been brought to the institution because she had taken a butcher knife to him. She had been there for some time and they thought she was getting along very well so they allowed him to go in and visit her. She again attempted to kill him right there on the spot. They asked me to come over and see what I could do. I don't know who recommended me or why. I went over and visited with the couple separately. Whenever she saw him she would just go into a rage. So I had prayer with her and rebuked the power of Satan. She was totally delivered from this obsession that she had. It was only a few days until they released her. She went back home with her husband, happy and blessed of the Lord. God really moved there in power.

Well, my friend who had stayed in Mankato decided it was time to get married. While he was on his honeymoon, his brother Harold came to take the church in Mankato. For some reason unknown to me the congregation didn't care for his brother and the church was closed up,all in two weeks. So Harold came to St. Peter and was going to hold evangelistic meetings at my new church and try to put ends back together. I went with him to Mankato and moved all the equipment out of the church and put it in storage until we could re-establish the church there. During this time our convention was being held in Rockford, Illinois so I went to the convention and left everything in the hands of Harold. I had scarcely arrived at the steps of the church when I was met by some of the leaders who said, "Charles, you've got to return immediately to St. Peter for they have arrested Harold. They have had his trial and he has been sentenced to a five year term in prison." "They have done what?" I queried. "That's right," came the reply. "They have accused him of stealing the equipment out of the church in Mankato." "That's impossible," I said. "For he wasn't the one that did it. I'm the one that took every piece out of the church and put it in storage. I took it!" "Well, for his sake and yours too, you had better go back there and see what you can do to get that poor soul out of jail," they said.

We paused, prayed and sought the will of God. Five ministers standing nearby decided that they would go with me. They all knew Harold and wanted to go and give a good word for him. They would also see that the situation would be backed with concentrated prayer. We got to St. Peter on Friday. I guess that was one of the quickest trials that had ever been held in Minnesota. We went directly that afternoon to the prosecuting attorney and the district attorney to see what we could find out and just what had happened. They gave us the story as they saw it. When they finished, I turned to them and said, "Let me tell you something. Harold had nothing to do with taking one piece of equipment out of that church. I am the one who took that equipment out and put it in storage waiting to re-establish another church

24

in Mankato. That congregation didn't like Harold and obviously some of them have it in for him. The things that were in that church didn't belong to the church. They were rightfully mine and I had the right to repossess them and put them in storage. I can show you all the receipts where I have purchased every single item they are accusing Harold of stealing from their church." At that the district attorney looked at me and said, "Mr. Robertson, that's not the story we were told." "I'm sorry sir, I can't help that. Let's get down to the facts," I answered. One by one we went through every documentation that I had received and I even showed them the receipt for the storage. "Gentlemen, Harold doesn't even know where the merchandise is. It is all intact and if you would like I will take you to the storage place and show it to you." I could see the perplexing look on both of the district attorney and the prosecuting attorney's faces. Almost simultaneously they said, "That boy has been falsely accused."

Poor Harold, he had come to court with only a few dollars in his pocket and when they threw him in jail, the inmates had a kangaroo court and decided to take all of his money. With it they bought some of the essentials they thought they needed. This was more serious than one can imagine. When he was convicted for a felony, he lost many of his citizenship rights. The district attorney decided that there should be another trial and it should be held at once. They rounded up a judge, got a jury and called a trial the very next morning, which was Saturday. Harold's initial trial and sentencing had been that fast and I suppose God in His mercy wanted his liberation to be just as quick. The trial was held and of course Harold was totally acquitted. The chief of police after the trial came around and took Harold off to the side and said, "Harold, we have a method of dealing with the fellow who accused you. We think we'll take him up to the hillside and work him over." Harold being a good Christian man, realized the overtones of what the chief of police intended and said, "No sir, I've been acquitted ard that's all that matters. I have forgiven him completely." I pitied the poor man who had accused Harold for it wasn't long before he had to leave the community because no one there would hire him. For some strange reason he wanted Harold to pay for the church's being broken up. Unfortunately you can be persecuted for Christ's sake without having done anything wrong.

Brother Bert and myself

Chapter Two

Gunda

My wife to be, or at least I was praying so, I don't think she was, went with another group to the Southwest to minister. We would go from city to city usually for about three months and establish a church and then we would turn it over to a person who was called to be its minister. It was our job to establish the core of the church. Gunda and I corresponded on quite a regular basis; however, it would be fourteen months before I would see her again.

We both returned to the Los Angeles area about the same time and soon we began dating. After several months of dating, I could not wait any longer and asked her to be my wife. I was expecting an immediate answer but Gunda looked at me and said, "Charles, I like you very much. As a matter of fact I believe I'm in love with you. But I have so many responsibilities at home. As you know my mother is deaf, and that would leave her all alone. I feel the responsibility of caring for her. You have just got to give me some time. I don't know as yet exactly what God would have me to do. Charles, I must claim Proverbs 3:5-6 which says, '*Trust in the Lord with all thine heart; and lean not unto thine own understanding. In all thy ways acknowledge Him, and He shall direct thy paths.*'"

Reluctantly, I agreed that it certainly would be in the will of the Father for us both to know what He would have us do. I claimed the verse in Matthew 6:33, "*Seek ye first the kingdom of God, and His righteousness: and all these things shall be added unto you.*"

After about two weeks had gone by, I looked Gunda in the eye and said, "Gunda, I strongly feel God would have you to be my wife and that we should spend our lives together ministering for the Lord Jesus. I also believe that if you take this step of faith, God will care for your mother and your little sister Catherina. I cannot take no for an answer."

I took the engagement ring out of my pocket and said, "I want you to have this ring."

At that remark Gunda tenderly looked at me and replied, "You are right, Charles, I will trust God. I love you and yes, I will marry you and serve the Lord with you."

At that I smiled and tenderly kissed her and placed the ring on her finger. We immediately began our wedding plans. We decided to be married on Christmas day in the evening at Angelus Temple.

I often wondered how Gunda got her name. Several years ago when we sent to Wendall, Idaho for Gunda's birth certificate, then I found out. We gave them her name and the date of her birth. They wrote back and stated, "We are sorry, we do not have a birth certificate for a Gunda Simonsen on that date but we do have a birth certificate for Catherina Simonsen." We then discovered that her name was Catherina.

When her father came home and gave his mother the news that a little girl had been born, he said, "Her name is Catherina." At that she began to cry. He said, "Mother, what's wrong?" She said, "Well, no one in the family has used my name or named any of their little girls after me." So he said. "Mother, don't you worry.

We will just call her Gunda." That's all there was to it! He never had it changed and it was just Gunda from then on. Gunda had always wondered, "Why did they ever name me Gunda? It is such a horrible name." As she got older and learned to know her grandmother she thought, "She is such a sweet person, I should never feel that way. It is an honor to have her name." Eleven years later another daughter was born and they named her Catherina also. So two in the same family are named Catherina.

We went to the court house and applied for our marriage license. Three days later after work, around 4:00 P.M., I went to the court house to pick up the license and to my shock and bewilderment all of the offices were closed. I forgot that the third day was Saturday.

I didn't know what to do. So I went home and prayed. I'll have to admit I did a little worrying also. I didn't say a word to Gunda. There was no use of her worrying, I was doing enough for both of us.

The next morning, Sunday, our wedding day and Christmas on top of it, I decided to start making phone calls to see if I could find a judge that would believe that I had applied for a license.

Call after call, I made the same desperate plea, "Please, please help me. My wedding is in eleven hours and I don't have a license." They would either laugh or give me a "no". Finally God surely intervened, for a judge asked me to come to his house and he would give me a paper of license to give to the pastor.

Needless to say, it did not take me very long to get to his home. He took a pencil from his desk and wrote on a piece of paper our permission to be married. When he handed it to me, I shouted, "Praise the Lord!"

At that he looked at me and simply said, "Congratulations, son, and Merry Christmas."

When I gave that piece of paper to the minister, she looked twice at it, but accepted it without comment.

An oratorio, *"The Bells of Bethlehem,"* had been

planned for the Christmas weekend. We made arrangements to be married at the conclusion of the oratorio. As a result the temple was decorated to the hilt. From the front platform there were two walkways ascending about twenty feet to two gardens, laden with flowers and greenery. One was called Mary's Garden and the other Elizabeth's Garden. Another walkway joined them at the top. The ramps were carpeted but because of the steep incline, they were very slippery especially for hard-soled shoes. I stood in one garden and Gunda walked the aisle and came up the ramp to join me. I was scared as I watched her come to me, for I was certain that she would slip and fall. She did do a bit of shuffling but made it fine.

Sister McPherson wasn't there so one of the other ministers married us. Because of the oratorio, we had over five thousand attend our wedding. Of course with that number there was no way that we could have any kind of reception.

At the time I was working for Woolworth's and Gunda was working at a cafeteria. That was in 1935. For the first month of our marriage we moved in with Gunda's mother. Then into our own apartment. We were not there long until we decided that we were called into the pioneer work of establishing churches for the Foursquare denomination.

Chapter Three

Learning From God

I had an old 1928 Chevy and when we got married, I had saved enough money that I could trade it in on a brand new 1935 Chevy coupe. The cost was a staggering $500. In those days that was staggering! The car even came equipped with one of the most fabulous radios that a car could contain at that time. It had the type of receiver on it that you could pick up stations many miles away.

We had very little money, but both of us decided that it was God's will that we go to Winslow, Arizona and establish a church. Soon after we arrived in Winslow, we met the most wonderful black couple. They were very spiritual and two of the finest people we have ever met. When it came to praying and intercession, that couple certainly knew how to pray and touch God. They also knew what it meant to stand behind Gunda and me with their prayers. We started having morning prayer meetings and that seemed to be the means by which God caused the church to grow.

After we were there for several weeks, we rented a

building just off the main street of town. It could seat about two hundred but we started with only a few families.

One day an elderly man came into the church simply to talk. During our conversation we discovered that he was sleeping in a barn with the animals. We invited him to sit down and warm himself. The next Sunday he was in our service. His family lived in Ohio, however, they considered him an outcast and would not have anything to do with him. I asked him if he would work if he had a job. "Yes," he said. "I would be glad to work if I could find something to do."

We had the congregation pray with him and then we gave him enough money so that he could have a warm room for the night. But he didn't rent a room and went right back to the barn. He is what we called in those days a railroad bum.

The next morning he got up and started down the street when a woman called and said, "Say, I need some help over here. Would you like to do some work for me? I need someone to take the ashes out. It would just be odds and ends around the house, it won't amount to much more than an hour a day. I will pay you well if you will do these things for me every day."

"Lady, if you will give me a place to stay, I will gladly do the work for you," he replied.

"We have struck up a bargain," she answered.

He then started his walk downtown. He had the "bed" money in his pocket and he decided to buy breakfast with it. He went into the restaurant and ordered his breakfast.

The owner walked up to him and said, "How would you like to wash dishes for me? I need someone right now."

"How did you know that I was looking for work?" the man asked him.

I just felt when you came in, you were going to ask me for work, so I simply thought that I would beat you to the punch."

Now he had his second job. He had a place to stay and a place to eat. He told everybody that when those people at that new church pray, things happen. So more people came. We seemed to have one experience after another like that.

The sheriff of the county brought a young boy to the church who was just barely twelve years old. I suppose he had brought him to us because his name was also Robertson. He asked us if we would take care of him. At the time we were in no position to take a young boy into our home as we were soon going to be moving on. We knew this boy needed stability in his life. He had run away from home because his parents were abusing and beating him. The poor little fellow had nothing to do but run or perhaps be killed. So again we went to prayer and asked God to provide this boy with a home.

It wasn't but hours until the sheriff came and said, "Well, I guess I'll just have to take him into my home and take care of him." He took him down town and bought him boots, a cowboy hat and all the clothes. The sheriff checked his story and the courts gave him custody and the sheriff agreed to raise him as his own. So again God answered our prayers. *"Suffer the little children to come unto Me and forbid them not: for of such is the kingdom of God."* Mark 10:14

To illustrate how marvelously and faithfully those servants of God prayed: We were asked to go to Albuquerque, New Mexico and pick up a huge revival tent for one of the evangelists. Of course the financial responsibility of getting there and returning was ours. We very rarely stayed in motels. We just drove and slept and drove and slept. The trip from Winslow to Albuquerque was several hundred miles. There were some mountains to go over and a desert to cross. Gunda always tried to stay awake and talk to me so I wouldn't go to sleep at the wheel. On our way to Albuquerque for reasons unknown to us we both fell asleep, and were heading for a very steep precipice. At the same time one of our faithful members was awakened by the Spirit of

God and began to intercede for us. She saw us heading over a mountain precipice and began praying and crying out to God to save our lives. At the same time my wife awakened and screamed, "Charles!" Instantly I turned the wheel of the car and we were saved from what would have been instant death, going over that mountain side. We couldn't help but pause and thank God for doing a miracle on our behalf

We continued on to Albuquerque and picked up the tent. On the way back I had not given my attention to the gas meter as I should have and about two o'clock in the morning, in the desert going up an incline, the car sputtered and came to a halt. "Gunda," I sheepishly said, "We've run out of gas." There doesn't seem to be any place in the world as desolate and lonely and dark as the desert at 2 o'clock in the morning. "Honey," I continued, "I've got to try to flag down a car or something and see if I can get a ride to the nearest gas station. I'll leave you here. Be sure to lock the car and whenever you see a car approaching turn the lights on so they'll know you are here and not hit you." We had prayer together and I got out to wave down a passing car. Of course there weren't many. Eventually I could see a large bus approaching. It did stop and gave me a ride. I'll never forget the terrible feeling I had as the bus pulled off and I left my wife in that desolate desert, alone. I knew however, she would trust God and that He would care for her. The bus let me off at a gas station. I pounded on the door until there was response. The man said, "Sure, I'll be glad to take you back to where your car is but before I can do anything I've got to have breakfast." Well, all I could think of was my wife there at the side of the road in the desert. So I prayed that God would keep her safe as this man slowly fried his bacon and eggs and made his toast. Then he sat down and began to eat his breakfast. I was so hungry I could hardly stand the suffering. It was all I could do to keep from showing my frustration, but then I had to be thankful for I was indeed at his mercy. It seemed like it wasn't too long till we pulled up along side the car, put the gas in the tank and we were on our way once again. As we pulled up to the gas station, I made a silent vow I would never again run out of gas. Believe me to this day forty-nine years later every time we drive any place Gunda will say, "Honey, how is the gas? Do you have enough?" So if I don't remember, my wife certainly will not let me forget that incident on the desert.

Charles "the groom"

My bride, Gunda

Chapter Four

Standing On The Word

It wasn't long after that, the call came for us to pastor a church in Kentucky. The church was established, there was a parsonage, running water and all. So we went there with great expectations. But along the way someone had forgotten to tell us that there had been three disastrous years of drought, crop failure, and that each family was allowed only one acre of money crop per person. If there was a family of three they could plant three acres. As we happily drove from Winslow to Kentucky, I wonder if our jubilation would have been as keen if we knew what was ahead. But, thank God, we walk with Jesus one day at a time.

My wife and I had never been to Kentucky and we knew nothing about the state of its people. It was a completely new field. We had for the most part lived in California, we had always lived in nice homes. Gunda's dad had always made good money and was never without anything. She always had clothes and every-thing the ordinary family would have. She wasn't used to baking biscuits for breakfast; they had a lovely bakery where they could buy their baked goods. Her home was a little above an ordinary home. We just wanted to be a blessing, to reach people and point them to the Lord. That was our entire aim. Not a big church, not a large salary, just to lead them to the Lord, was the greatest challenge we had before us.

I didn't think we would ever find the town. We drove in with our coupe and on to a country road. They had just had a real gully wash as the road was covered with water. We all know that dirt and water make mud. We started down the road as directed. At first we couldn't find the city of Livia, for it was only a sign and railroad Everywhere we would ask they would say that it was back in the hills. Directions in "the hills" are mostly barns, trees, and fences. All our worldly possessions were in that coupe. We had a few linens, dishes, towels, and two cooking pans. We started down the road and you could see the fresh wagon ruts. We got to a place where we couldn't go backward or forward, we were stuck down to our axles and it was dark. Gunda said,"Charles, what are we going to do now?" We sat in the car just to think and of course to pray. Pretty soon, way down the road, we saw people walking with a lantern.

"Hello! Hello!",they called. I yelled back, "We're looking for the church." "We're the church, young man," they replied. We of course left the car in the mud and walked in mud and water to a very nice country home where nice people put us up for the night. Early in the morning before we were really ready to get up, about 6 a.m., we were called to breakfast. We quickly dressed and enjoyed a nice southern breakfast consisting of: bacon, eggs, biscuits, gravy and grits.

After breakfast, the kind people that we had spent the

night with asked us if we would like to get settled into the parsonage. Of course Gunda was rather anxious and I certainly was also. They told us we could return later and they would help us get our car out of the mud. We did, however, go to the car and get a few of our belongings and piled them on the horse-drawn wagon. It was quite an experience getting ourselves up into the wagon and making our way up the old country road bouncing in and out of the ruts on our way to our new home. We were told that everything was furnished with running water and all so we were really expecting something quite nice. When we got to the end of the lane the only thing we saw was an old shed.

I questioningly said, "What is that?" The man simply replied, "Why that is your new home. We've taken an old tobacco shed and fixed it up for you. I think quite nice, too. I think it will do you quite well." My eyes flew open as I looked from one side to the other. There were no sidewalks, little plank boards for steps. The sides of the house were made with plank boards oftentimes spaced two and three inches apart. That was done intentionally to let air through to dry the tobacco leaves. I quickly noticed that there was no outhouse either.

Gunda and I went in first and there we saw our furniture. An old bedstead on one side of the room, a straight chair or two and in the kitchen was an old dilapidated cast iron stove. There also was a table covered with chicken droppings that showed who obviously were the occupants of this "beautiful home." There was a pie cupboard also. Gunda simply looked around and said, "I have a table cloth I believe in my suitcase that will fit quite nicely on that table." "Honey, where is the bathroom, I don't see one anyplace?" I whispered back, "Gunda, I don't believe there is one, inside or out." It became quite obvious that there was no running water inside the house so I questioningly asked, "Where do we get our water?" They answered, "Oh, you'll have to walk down this road about an eighth of a mile, cross the barbed wire fence and up on top of the hill there, there's a home and they'll just be more than happy to let you have all the water you want from their fresh spring; you'll love that water too." At that our new friends left and we stood there amazed as we heard the wagon bounce in and out of those dirt ruts and soon the sound faded out of our ears. We stood there and looked in total amazement at each other, chuckled a little and realized that God had sent us here, so we would make it.

We were thirsty and decided our first task would be to get some water to drink and some to try and straighten up the kitchen table. We looked around for a bucket but there was none so all we had to carry water in was a small one-quart pan and the other pan was a quart and a half. So that's what we had for drinking water, wash water, dish water; everything that required water had to be carried in those two small pots. We had no skillets and so for the first week or so the pickings were slim. We both knew we were going to make it and we were going to work hard at it. We started out down the lane to get water, climbed over the barbed wire fence and up the hill and there it was just like they said a fresh running spring. We filled the pans and headed back down the hill. We were progressing along quite well when all of a sudden Gunda came to an abrupt stop. As a matter a fact, started backing up. "Charles, Charles!" was all she could exclaim. "What's wrong, Gunda, what's wrong?" I asked. "The, the, the, the road is full of snakes," she stammered. I fixed my eyes on the road and sure enough as far as I could see in every rut and indention in the road there was a snake curled. They were all out sunning themselves. We'd take several steps forward and one back and then we prayed. We decided we just had to walk between them and so we did. They just stayed there sunning themselves for which we were very grateful. They weren't little, either; they were big fat round ones. I suppose in that eighth of a mile we did more intensive praying than we had in a long time. We didn't have any soap or rags so we really couldn't clean the table that night and we didn't eat off of it needless to say, either.

Some of the church folks had given us a pounding. That means that they gave us a pound of beans, a pound of rice, a pound of this and a pound of that. In reality, it was a grocery shower; however, it was all food that Gunda would have to cook on the stove and that meant that I would have to go out and cut wood. There was an axe there and when I went to use it, it bounded higher than the indention in the wood. Try as I would, I could scarcely cut it so I had to break it and pick up some pieces. It was something that they called iron-wood and to this day you can't convince me that it wasn't as hard as iron. We finally got our things together for the first night. We were so tired and exhausted that the bed even at its worst looked mighty nice. I thought any moment Gunda would start crying, but she wasn't a woman to cry, she just became more determined than ever to make the best of it.

I can remember her turning to me that night and saying, "Why, Charles, look at how bad it must have been for the pioneers and if they could do it, we can do it." Our light was a coal oil lantern; it was lit and glowing and I held it as Gunda pulled back the covers preparing the bed for our night's sleep. Much to our amazement, the sheets were covered with bed bugs, not one or two and I might be exaggerating when I say it was wall to wall but it certainly might just as well have been. Not only did the bed bugs come out at night, but we heard varments, it seemed like of every description, running around in the attic above us. Then Gunda saw one; a big rat scurried across one of the beams. That did it!

She went to the bedstand, got the Bible, laid it on the old plank floor and said, "Now, Charles, there is nothing else for us to do. We have to stand on this Bible literally and claim it cover to cover." So there we were, two people trying to get four feet on the Bible. But we stood on it and we prayed, "Lord, You've taken care of us before, You care for the missionaries, You've cared for many people in hard places. Now in Jesus' name we ask You to care for us. Remove from this house the bedbugs

41

and the rats and the snakes and the wasps, and, Lord Jesus, we stand on your Word and we claim it from cover to cover. We claim the 91st Psalm as our own, this night." Then we began to quote it:

"He that dwelleth in the secret place of the most High shall abide under the shadow of the Almighty. I will say of the Lord, He is my refuge and my fortress: my God; in Him will I trust. Surely He shall deliver thee from the snare of the fowler, and from the noisome pestilence. He shall cover thee with His feathers, and under His wings shalt thou trust: His truth shall be thy shield and buckler. Thou shalt not be afraid for the terror by night; nor for the arrow that flieth by day; nor for the pestilence that walketh in darkness; nor for the destruction that wasteth at noonday. A thousand shall fall at thy side and ten thousand at thy right hand; but it shall not come nigh thee. Only with thine eyes shalt thou behold and see the reward of the wicked. Because thou hast made the Lord, which is my refuge, even the most High, thy habitation; there shall no evil befall thee, neither shall any plague come nigh thy dwelling. For He shall give His angels charge over thee, to keep thee in all thy ways. They shall bear thee up in their hands, lest thou dash thy foot against a stone. Thou shalt tread upon the lion and adder: the young lion and the dragon shalt thou trample under feet. Because he hath set his love upon Me, therefore will I deliver him: I will set him on high because he hath known My name. He shall call upon Me, and I will answer him: I will be with him in trouble; I will deliver him, and honour him. With long life will I satisfy him, and shew My salvation."

We believed it or we wouldn't have done it. We believed that God would rid the road of the snakes, the house of the bugs, rats and wasps and He did! The rats never came into the house, we heard them but they never came down into the house. The bedbugs disappeared, they were completely gone. We could stand in the middle of the floor and see the ground below or the stars above. We had air conditioning all around as many of the vertical slats in the walls were not there.

Our first Sunday there we were invited out to dinner. The people lived about a quarter of a mile down the road. They were lovely people. The husband was eighty-four and he walked ten miles to his work and ten miles back every morning and every night. He worked on the W.P.A. The grandson stayed home and worked the field. He had worked the horse so hard that it fell over dead. I felt so sorry for this old couple. They had been flooded out for three years in succession. They were still willing to share what they had with us and they invited us for dinner. We each had a small dish of beans, a piece of fatback, a biscuit and a glass of clabbered milk. It was thick clabber! They were really poor folk, but shared the widow's mite with us.

"Charles," Gunda remarked, "If they were willing to share that which they needed so badly themselves we should always remember to pray for them."

They were special people. Anything they could do to help us they were more than happy to do.

One day some folks came to see us. We were so new and green, we were like foreigners and somewhat suspect. While they were visiting, the lady kept talking about her son being such a crack shot with guns. They challenged me to go out and see what I could do with his gun. We went outside and they pointed at a bird. I took his gun and prayed, "God, help me," and shot. I hit that bird right in the middle of its head. The bird fell to the ground then the little fellow went over, picked up the bird and said nothing. After that they never came over and challenged me about guns again. They had also tried to scare us, by telling us about how many people had been killed in "our" house.

Most of the people had only two pair of jeans. An old

pair and once a year they would get a new pair. They could only buy their shoes and their pair of jeans when their crop came in, so they had to make do. They were very poor, but they were people who loved God and they were hungry for His Word. Most of the church members had a genuine love for the Lord; however, there were also some who were moonshiners. But tobacco was their main crop. If the crop was perfect, they made $60.00 an acre. So they never had any money left over.

The church was a brand new building. I know there were many sacrifices made to build it. It was about thirty feet by forty feet. It had a nice floor and would seat about two hundred people. It had nice home-made benches and a lovely pulpit. When those people came, the church was full and when they sang, they sang like a Heavenly Choir. Gunda often said to me, "It was a pleasure for us to be sent to a place like that, because the people knew how to have church." They knew the Lord and loved Him very much; you could tell it by the way they sang except when they "laughed."

The fall season was fast approaching and as there was no electricity, before the service was over, we had to light the kerosene lamps. The wasps had started coming in from the cool outside and when I lit one of the lamps, I didn't notice it but the wasps started pouring out of it. I was sitting there trying to be calm but they were climbing all over my back, my neck and my ears. Gunda was leading the singing and the congregation started to snicker. I noticed her look around trying to find something wrong but she was determined to go right ahead. The more I swatted them off of me the harder the congregation laughed. I could tell she was becoming more and more perplexed because the congregation was almost hysterical as they watched me trying to deliver myself from the wasps before I began to preach. When she sat down after the song service and they were still snickering she had no idea what had been going on but before the service was over, in my message I clued her in. Not one stung me but they did bite. A wasp will let you

44

know when they are around so our first service was one of joy and laughter. One bright sunshiny Sunday morning, Gunda said, "I'm going to get my red satin blouse out and I'll feel better." As we were walking down the road to church, we noticed how the trees were over hanging us and what a pretty lane it was. As we walked along in the middle of that lane I heard a loud thumping. We couldn't figure out what that noise was. Finally Gunda looked up on the hill and said, "Honey, there's a cow coming." I yelled, "That's no cow, that's a bull! Get behind the tree quick." She couldn't figure out why she should get behind a tree. He was really aggravated and coming down over that hill fast. The bull finally turned and went the other way and we hurried home so Gunda could change her blouse.

By this time we were pretty hungry. The food was sparse. We would rather go without than tell the people. We couldn't fix much on that stove as the pipe was laid in a hole in the wall and served as the chimney. As a result there was no draft to cause the fire to burn. I filled the cracks in the stove with mud. It would take about two hours to bake the biscuits so they were always like brick bats.

The offerings were about $1.00 a month. So that meant our salary was $3.00 for the entire three months. We were grateful for the opportunity, but finally a lady came along that would live with the people. I told the District Superintendent that it would be better to have someone that knew their ways and knew them to be their pastor.

So after she came, I wrote to the organization and asked for another opening.

We were health-wise run down by now. While we waited, we went to Pennsylvania. My mother, aunt, and children were going there to visit relatives, so we thought it might be a good idea to go there, see them, rest up before we took over another church. We only had a few dollars so we took sandwiches. Gunda went in a store for additional food and bought a bag of pretzels.

Bless her heart, that was something she was so hungry for. Nothing she brought out was anything I wanted, but I ate it anyway. When we got up to Ohio, we thought we'd stop to see friends and they weren't home. They were traveling. I felt impressed of God to go to the Post Office while I was there. When I asked if we had any mail, there was a letter from Gunda's mother, General Delivery. In that letter was $10. Gunda said, "Praise the Lord," and I amened her. Her mother didn't know where we were or that we needed money but God did, so He had her send it! The first thing we did was go out and get a good meal. We got a dish of Blue Pike and that was the best fish I believe I have ever eaten. We then continued on to Pennsylvania. On the way I stopped the car and said, "I'm going to have to step out here, I'll be right back." I pulled off the road and went back in the woods to relieve myself. When I came back after a very long time I asked Gunda, "Why didn't you come looking for me?" She said, "I didn't know where you went." "Honey, I passed out. I have a high fever and I'm very sick," I mumbled.

Gunda said, "Let's drive to the first motel we come to and stay there over night." We didn't have very much money but we had enough to stay at the motel overnight. I believe the room then cost $4.00. The next morning we got up and continued on to Pennsylvania. I was still very sick. Gunda could not drive very well, so I was still driving. When we got to my aunt's, I broke out with a heavy case of shingles. I mean they were terrible. I was in bed for almost three weeks with a high fever. Evidently we were more exhausted than we realized. They did, however, disappear with rest.

While we were resting, we thought it would be a good idea to go up on top of the hill near my aunt's place, where there was a small settlement, and hold some children's meetings. The adults also came and before long we had almost one hundred coming to the services. We held them for about two months and then we felt we should go back to California.

Chapter Five

Concord And Belmont

We were in California about three months, fully rested, and we decided we were ready to take on our next ministry. We were asked to go to the city of Concord, North Carolina and take over a tabernacle that would seat 2,300 people. There was a beautiful apartment in the complex and we were assured that this would be not quite as strenuous as our last assignment. There were several things, however, we were not told. It was true the tabernacle would seat 2,300 people and there was a nice apartment but when we got there, we discovered all the windows had been boarded up and the congregation was scattered. There was a debt on the church and the contents. The unpaid light, gas, and coal bills were beyond belief. The situation in the natural was totally impossible. It was devastating to us when we realized the complexities of the situation we now found ourselves in. The foreclosure of the property had already been finalized.

The church in Concord known as Elizabeth Temple was right on U.S. Highway 29 which was the main route from Florida to New York. In that day it was more important than Highway 1. Elizabeth Temple was known from Florida to New York by people who had travelled that route because it was such a famous place. People would stop there for services whenever they were going through. It was patterned after Angelus Temple in California. The type of services that they held were very similar. So it had a great reputation yet when it got into its legal difficulties, it totally closed up. If that Foursquare church failed, the whole seaboard would have failed. The temple was, more or less, the backbone for the church in Norfolk and all the churches on up the coast. So it was very important that this church carry on.

Oh, there were times that I could have become very angry and upset for having been sent there and not told the entire situation. Gunda and I realized, however, we were in God's hands and we would simply make the best of it and see what God would do for us. We were certain that God was only preparing us for something else and this was going to be a stepping stone. Even though I felt we had been deceived, I knew God was on the throne. How I thank God that He had already seasoned me or I would have become disillusioned at that point with the organized church.

It was November and therefore it had started turning cold and we needed coal to heat the church. Everything seemed to be against us. For the next thirteen weekends we had nothing but rain or snow. The income of the people at that time was very low, about $7.00 a week, and there simply wasn't money. We believed God for a miracle and started services. At our first service there were only twenty-two people. There were three ministers who had sued each other and the court ruled that one would preach one Sunday, and another the next Sunday and the third one would preach the third Sunday. So there were like three different congregations. They were all independent Pentecostal and the Foursquare sent us, with God's help to bring unity.

48

To add to all of our stress, Gunda was expecting our first child. She always seemed to have peace during the storms of life.

We had had our services downstairs and we had gone upstairs to our apartment about 12 p.m. Gunda suddenly shouted, "Charles, see the flash of lightning outside!" At that all of our lights went out. At that time, Bert, my brother, and his wife Mary were staying with us, helping with the ministry. Bert and I went downstairs to the Crusade room and someone had gotten in there and put wet saw dust up the light socket. That had blown the fuses. We had to work by lamp trying to figure out what was wrong. About two o'clock in the morning, the same night, we had to call the doctor. Gunda had gone into labor. He came, checked Gunda and went to check on some other ladies in labor and then several hours later came back. Bert walked the floor with a cup of coffee all night long. We had a wonderful German doctor, the kind who would come to the home. Finally the baby came and it was a boy! So we named him Charles after me. After Charles was born, I said, "Doctor, how much do I owe you?" Of course in those days you told the doctor you were expecting and that was the last you saw of him until the day the baby came. The doctor asked, "How much do you have in your pocket?" I replied, "Ten dollars." The doctor said, "We'll just charge you $10 for that boy then." He was the best baby you have ever seen. You would never know you had a baby around the house. He never cried. He was always happy. He was one of those babies that when he was four months old he looked like he was a year old. Always smiling. He grew fast.

The tabernacle had always been surrounded with mystery. Time after time strange happenings would take place. I remember the time when we had an evangelist staying with us. He was occupying the back bedroom. For anyone to get back to that bedroom they had to go through our bedroom. All of the rooms were in one long row. He awakened and there was a man in his room jumping up and down carrying on and screaming as though he was going to kill the evangelist. The windows were screened and there was absolutely no way for anyone to have gotten to that room without our knowing it. He was so frightened he was determined not to stay one more night in that house without a body guard. And believe it or not, he hired one. We had no logical explanation for what had happened unless it was a satanic attack.

During that revival we had many converts and one that stood out was a man that was a candy maker. In the middle of the service he came to the altar even while the evangelist was still preaching. We dealt with the man and he accepted the Lord. After the service he told us that he had been in bed and someone had knocked on his door. As he got up and answered the door a voice said, "You've got to give your heart to the Lord Jesus tonight." He dressed, came to our church, walked down the aisle and accepted Christ.

Night after night we would hear footsteps coming up the stairs from the church. There were twenty-two steps up to our apartment. We would sit in our living room many times with my brother and sister-in-law and we would hear the step 1, 2, 3. . . When the footsteps would almost be to the top, I would get up slowly, go to the door and quickly open it and there would never be anyone there. I suppose there were over fifty different people who had heard the footsteps on those steps and never saw anyone.

One time we came home and all the doors were locked from the inside. I had to crawl through the coal chute and make my way through the darkness to open the door. Our keys were no good with the doors locked and bolted from the inside.

We had a very active young peoples' group at the church. It was a very unique one. We would give them questions on one Sunday and they would bring the answers back the following Sunday. They wanted to study the Bible and they wanted to find God. So it wasn't an imposition to them to study, it was something they wanted to do. When they couldn't find the answer they would go to the ministers of the other churches and ask them what their answer was. So it got the whole ministerial alliance involved and all stirred up. One Presbyterian minister told us he had gone to seminary, but he had never learned any of this. It so challenged and impressed him that he had to give his heart to the Lord. "Here I've been preaching for years and I'm not a Christian," he said. Not only did he give his heart to the Lord but he resigned the church and started a new one. When you get the young people asking questions about the Bible, you stir up a lot of people. It united the ministers because they discovered in answering these questions that they were all fundamentalists in their thinking. They began to meet at this new church every week and have a Bible Study. It was a thrilling thing, because it gave them a unity that they didn't have before.

Nevertheless we knew that we had a big God. We did fill the building for a week when little Charles James the child evangelist came to preach. There were so many people there the fire marshall made us close the doors to keep others from coming in. After those meetings were over, the bank sold the church. After the bills were paid there was about $5,000 left. I wrote to headquarters asking what I should do with the money. They told me to take the money and forget the church! I, of course, couldn't do that. I took the money and bought some property around the corner from the temple. We built the church so the front was like a lighthouse even with the light revolving around in it. We called it THE FOURSQUARE LIGHTHOUSE. It wasn't long before our congregation began to grow. The ones who had left were now beginning to come back.

Our apartment was in the basement of the new church with steps leading up to the sanctuary. Gunda was now expecting our second child.

I will never forget the morning that she went into labor. It was just before Sunday morning worship service. I had sent for the doctor but for some reason he had taken a long time getting there. So I rushed upstairs to get two of the ladies of the church, Mrs. Sides and Mrs. Sellers, so that they could come downstairs and care for Gunda. Finally the time came where the congregation was waiting for the preacher and Gunda insisted that I go on upstairs and handle the work of the Lord. Let me tell you, that was some morning. In between the singing and the preaching, we could hear Gunda crying out in her labor. I thought that I would never make it through the sermon and neither would the congregation. I could tell with every noise that Gunda made we, especially the women, were in labor with her. Finally we heard the cry of the baby and all of us gave a sigh of relief.

I hurried downstairs as quickly as I could to find out whether I had another son or a daughter. Much to my delight our daughter, Brittarose, was born. It was Palm Sunday, so I had more than one reason for singing HALLELUJAH!

I couldn't help overhearing the women saying to Gunda, "Oh, Gunda, that baby is not going to live. Look how yellow she is. She has jaundice." They were scaring my wife to death and me, too. We decided, right then and there, to claim a victory of healing for little Brittarose. It was only a matter of a day or two before her skin cleared up and we realized that we had a very healthy baby. Even though she couldn't drink milk like a normal baby, she continued to grow and turned into a fine child. It was a hardship, for in those days, there were no formulas that we could give to her. Also in that apartment our daughter Nellie Darlene was born.

All of our children were dedicated within hours of their birth. It seemed interesting how God would bring another pastor along just in time to dedicate them. I never dedicated my own children except in the fact that Gunda and I always dedicated them before God even before they were born.

Gunda was a very strong woman and could do about anything in the church to help me. One of the nights that I was preaching I noticed the girl who was living with us, who had problems at home, leave the meeting. She had gone downstairs to check on the children. As she opened the door, she saw a large black snake go into the bedroom. She told the children to get on the bed. So there they were, all screaming, we could hear it upstairs, and Gunda went down to see what was wrong. Gunda grabbed a broom and every time she hit the snake the children would scream and the snake would strike. It was a cottonmouth water moccasin, a very deadly one. Gunda made mincemeat out of it. However, that was not the end of the snakes. There were several babies that were just as deadly as the mother also in the bedroom. They tell us that the venom of the baby snake is just as deadly as that of the adult. They had, however, the same fate as their mother. Sometime later we bought a parsonage across the street from the church.

There were some people from the town of Belmont, about forty miles away from Concord, that wanted us to begin a work there. We bought a tent that would seat about two hundred people.

One of the men and I decided that we would put this tent up by ourselves. Neither one of us had ever put up a tent before. We were very successful, at first. We got the canvas almost up and a thunderstorm hit. Not only did the tent come down, but it came down on us. It filled with water so quickly that the weight of the water brought us right down too. By the time that we got out from under the tent we thought that we would be crushed-to-death. But after persevering, we finally got the tent up. We had ordered in some lumber to make a platform and some benches. Some of the men from the cotton mill came along when they were changing shifts and I thought that they were going to heckle us or pick a fight. Instead, they asked when we were going to start the meetings. We told them that we would probably start Sunday if we could get everything built on time.

The rain started to pour again. I told them that if they would help us, we would start as soon as the benches and platform were built. They said, "We'll be back right after our shift is over and we will help." Praise God, they returned and worked.

So I had a lot of rough help, good wood butchers. We built the platform and benches and started the meetings on Friday night. This was a town where they had all kinds of fights for entertainment. It was not uncommon for them to kill somebody on a Saturday night. We had a good crowd right from the beginning and the Lord worked in a beautiful way. Many, many, were converted.

I drove back and forth from Concord to Belmont every day, eighty miles round trip, driving into the sun going and the headlights coming home. The sun and lights really worked on my eyes. That was before we knew much about polaroid glasses. It was nine weeks that we went steadily every day. By that time it was getting cold and we had put kerosene heaters in the tent. Finally, it was getting too cold and I said that we would have to shut down. I hadn't been able to find a room or building in which to continue the meetings. Some ladies came to me one night and said, "Would you be willing to use the women's club house?" I said, "I would be delighted to. I tried to rent it before and they wouldn't let me." "We'll take care of that if you will just continue. We have it for every night," the women replied. So every night I returned. That meant that on Wednesday night prayer meetings and Sunday night church services at Concord, Gunda would be in charge. She led the song service and preached.

While we were still in the tent, the ministers all decided to get together and come over and study our procedures. Then they would preach on Sunday morning and expose me. On Friday night we had a full tent. The sides were up and people were all around the tent on the outside. I noticed a row of people that looked different, but then I didn't give it another thought. We went right into the service, we didn't even get out of the song service and people were coming down to the altar to be saved, others were receiving the baptism of the Holy Spirit. It was just wonderful. It became one of those services that you didn't have control of, God did. People were also healed.

A boy standing to the side with his bicycle was being preached to by one of our girls. She was about sixteen and preaching him a sermon in tongues, it was tremendous. He threw his bicycle down and came and threw himself at the altar. He couldn't understand all the words he was hearing; he must have been hearing something. He was sobbing as he accepted Jesus Christ as his Saviour.

Here these ministers, about ten o'clock, got up and left. I noticed that other men took their places. The service went on till about midnight. There wasn't even a collection. So those ministers didn't have anything to preach about the following Sunday. The Lord just took care of them.

The pastor of the First Baptist Church came to me several days later and told me what their purpose had been in being there. He said that he wanted to invite me to be his assistant pastor. Of course I said, "Thank you, but God has called me to a different work."

We certainly loved the people in the Belmont and Concord churches even though it meant my being gone all week. We couldn't help but stand back and marvel at how God moved in those churches. The congregations were just beautiful and the people absorbed the Word of God.

In the various churches we started God did marvelous things for those congregations. One of the young men in Concord was a conscientious objector and filed such with the local draft board. As a result, they were going to put him in prison. So I went to the draft board with him and talked to them. They consented to put him in a non-combat position as a medic. Several years later when the war was over, he came to me and said, "Brother Robertson, I vowed I'd never kill anybody. But I had to break my vow during the war. I was treating the wounded on the field, when an enemy soldier came out of nowhere to kill us. I grabbed a nearby gun and without thinking twice, shot him. What's God going to do to me now? I killed him!" Well, it wasn't easy to explain to him that what he had done was all right. After much talking and praying, he finally came to realize that he had chosen right. He hadn't taken a life because he wanted to; it was forced on him. There is a difference between killing and murder.

One of the most outstanding conversions in my ministry took place at Belmont. The church was packed to capacity. I gave the invitation for those wanting salvation, prayer, healing, etc. Many came to the altar. Suddenly I looked up and here came a man weeping, jumping on the backs of the seats, to the altar. He couldn't get there any other way so I mean he literally came to the altar from back to back on the benches. "I want Jesus as my Saviour and now," he cried. We of course prayed with him and almost instantly you could see the change come over his face. A few days later he came and told me that he was an escapee from prison. "Preacher," he said, "This is the first time I've ever had peace that I can remember. I know that Jesus wants me to go back to prison in Georgia and serve my time." I asked him if he wanted somebody to go with him and he said, "No, it was my sin and I have to pay the price." The church went to prayer asking God to deliver him. When the time came for his hearing, there were scores of letters and telegrams there that had been written by many of the towns' people in his defense. The warden and the governor had heard all about how he'd been living since he had been saved. After they went through all this procedure of a hearing, etc., they let him go. The warden arranged his pardon. The Lord truly honored him for his determination to do what was right before God. He had escaped from a chain gang. So this was a real miracle. He had twin daughters who also accepted

Jesus and to this very day serve God. Needless to say there was a lot of rejoicing in our church over his complete pardon.

Another instance of God's miraculous intervention that comes to my mind is the case of the little girl in our church that was about six years old. During the winter we received an urgent call from the girl's grandmother to come quickly to her home. Her granddaughter was so sick that they were afraid that death was imminent.

It had been raining and sleeting hard and all the streets and sidewalks were nothing but a glaze of ice. We felt that we must go, and go immediately. I didn't realize how treacherous it was. I had on hard soled shoes and it seemed like every step that I took I would either slide or fall. We had three blocks to walk and I really didn't know if I could make it or not without crushing my skull. Gunda seemed to keep her feet better than I. I thought for sure, at times, that I would have to get on my hands and knees and literally crawl and before we got there, I did just that!

When we finally arrived, the doctor had already been there. He had told the parents that the girl had a severe case of scarlet fever. There was nothing that they could do but wait it out. We went to the bed and our eyes confirmed that the girl was in serious trouble. Without a miracle she would never last until morning. We opened our vial of oil and poured some on her head. We prayed the prayer of faith as we were told to do in the Scriptures. We claimed in the name of Jesus that the healing would be hers. We stayed for awhile and then decided that it would be best that we go home and try to get some sleep. It was a miracle that we ever made our way home. The next day the mother called us and was absolutely full of jubilation as she told us how her daughter's fever had broken and that she was perfectly well. As a matter of fact, the mother told us that she had just let her go out to play in the snow. All we could do was give God the glory and honor for His miracle. For He alone was the only source of this girl's deliverance.

We ministered in Concord and Belmont for eight years. Then God showed us it was time to leave.

A friend and myself at St. Peter

My brother, Bert

Gunda's brother and sister, Sonny and Kay

Chapter Six

The Midnight Angel

When we left the Belmont and Concord churches, I was down to 121 pounds and Gunda was more or less just skin and bone. I went to the doctor and he said, "Look, Charles, if you want to carry on and raise your family," at that time we had three children, "you're going to have to leave the ministry for awhile. If you don't, you won't be here to raise them." So I felt that for the family's sake I would have to slow down.

We knew for certain because of our health and tiredness we needed to return to California. Not only for a rest, but to wait upon God to see what He would have us to do next. We sold our 1939 Dodge because we knew that with our ration stamps there was no way we would have enough gas to get us all the way to California. We decided we would take a bus for that was, at that time, the cheapest way to travel. So there was Gunda, myself and three children. Charles was perhaps five at the time, and Brittarose three and Darlene was just a baby. We got as far as El Paso, Texas and were told that we were being bumped for service men. Which simply meant that we would have to stay in El Paso until there were five vacancies on a bus. I couldn't believe my ears. We had very little money and when the dispatcher said that we would be there for five days and we had better stay right at the bus station for when the call came we would have to be available to board the bus immediately, I looked at Gunda with total despair. I didn't know how we would survive five days in the El Paso bus terminal. It was wall to wall people. Our suitcases had been checked through to California so we only had the clothes that were on our backs. There was nothing else we could do. So again we committed the situation to God. We were hungry. We decided to go to a nearby restaurant and each have one good meal, which would surely lift our spirits. One of the dishes that was served to us was zucchini squash. I had never eaten it before and even liked the taste of it. But little beknown to me, as I was eating it, the skin was poisoning me. It wasn't long after the meal was finished that my body began to swell and I became sick unto death. We had returned to the bus depot and were sitting on the benches. I turned to Gunda and said, "Honey, something is radically wrong with me, I think you had better call an ambulance. I feel as though I might die." At that I took my billfold and handed it to her and said, "Here, you keep this."

By the time the men got there in the ambulance I was almost delirious, I couldn't walk, I was staggering, everything was incoherent and I could scarcely talk. They thought I was drunk, because I was vomiting everywhere. They soon discovered I was sick and in a very serious condition. I was then rushed to the hospital. Poor Gunda, there she was with three kids alone in a bus station and her husband enroute to the hospital. She had presence of mind to call California and ask the Christians there to be in earnest prayer for me. My mother promised that calls would go out and that people would pray. As the ambulance was tearing down the road enroute to the hospital, they went over a railroad track and it literally bounced me a foot off the cot. As I hit the cot again, I thought that everything in me was going to split. They rushed me into the emergency room. The doctor looked at me and immediately said, "Mr. Robertson, we're going to operate!" The nurse standing by looked at him so out of character and said, "Doctor, you can't do that. His wife isn't here and you can't operate on him without her permission." I didn't know how she knew I had a wife unless the ambulance driver had told her I left a wife and three kids back at the bus station. She seemed so insistent that the doctor paused and was taken back somewhat and turned to me and said, "Sir, what do you want me to do?" In my incredible pain I looked up to him and said, "Doctor, do anything you want to do. All I know is I can't stand this pain." The nurse again said, "You can't operate, not without his wife's permission." For a few minutes there seemed to be a battle raging. I didn't know where I was and quite frankly I didn't even care. I laid there for several hours. About three o'clock in the morning the pain seemed to subside and I somewhat came to my senses. I raised up on the bed on my elbows and realized I was in a prison-like cell. At that the nurse came rushing in to the room. "Mr. Robertson, everything's all right. We had a race riot in town last night and the only place we had to put you was in the hospital prison ward. I've been standing very close to you all night watching your every movement. "How do you feel now?" she asked, "How do I feel now?" I questioned, "Well I'm rational so I must be feeling somewhat better, but I certainly know I am not a well man." "But you are feeling better?" again she questioned. I said, "Well, yes."

"Mr. Robertson," she continued, "The doctor will be in about 5 o'clock this morning and he is going to want to operate. I'm going to be here when he arrives. I'll bring you some water. I want you to wash your face and look as fresh and healthy as you can and tell him that you're feeling fine." I thought to myself, "What in the world is wrong with this nurse? Why does she want me to pretend and put on this act?" Of course, little did I realize that Gunda had called Angelus Temple and my mother. Everybody was claiming my healing. About 4:30 in came the nurse with my water and she said to me, "Soon after the doctor leaves I'm going to bring your clothes to you. Put them on and we'll get you out of here. Don't you dare let him know I'm doing this!" When the doctor came in and said, "Mr. Robertson, are you ready for surgery?" I looked up and said, "Surgery? No, not till my wife Gunda gets here." At that he wrote a script and gave the nurse orders that I was to drink this medication. He said that at eight o'clock I would be ready for surgery. I didn't know exactly what it was, but the nurse did follow his instructions. I drank the entire glass of medication. It looked like milk of magnesia. I gulped it down and the doctor seemed satisfied. He had no more than left, when the nurse came in with my clothes. "I've talked to the head nurse and just as soon as you get dressed go down to her office. I have already arranged for your release."

She told me where the office was and at that left the room. I couldn't walk very well, but I did so leaning on the wall. I was so sick and I thought the nurse was crazy, but she was so insistent that I simply did what she said. I got to the head nurse's office. She looked at me and said, "Mr. Robertson I've been waiting for you. All the papers are in order and we are ready for your release." "I have no money, how can I leave without paying you?" I asked. "Oh, Mr. Robertson, that's all been cared for, the bill is totally paid for," she answered. "How on earth am I ever going to get back to the bus station?" I queried. With such matter of factness that it startled me, she said, "You go out in front of the hospital and you take street car number 223. Now you wait for 223, don't take the first car because that will not get you to the bus station." My face flushed a little as I turned to her and I said, "Ma'am, I don't have a penny with me." "Oh," she said and reached into her pocket and gave me some money. I still couldn't quite comprehend what was happening. I was still very sick. I went out on the street and let the first street car pass me by and then got on number 223. It took me directly to the bus station. The other nurse had just simply disappeared; I never saw her again. Believe me, my ride on the street car was a much better one than I had in the ambulance.

As I entered the bus station, the fellow at the ticket window said, "Mister, come over here. Aren't you the fellow that they took to the hospital last night?" I said, "Yes, I am." "Get your family together," he said. "You've been cleared for the next bus out!" "Do you know where my wife is?" I questioned. At that another man stepped up and said, "Sir, I do. She's in my room. I gave her and the children my room." So I went to the room where he told me she would be and sure enough there she was. She had washed the children's clothes out and now was in the process of trying to get them dried. When she first saw me, she almost fainted. I said, "Gunda, hurry up, get the children dressed. We're due out on the next bus!" There was nothing to do but put the wet clothes on the children, gather them up and rush downstairs to the waiting bus. With wet clothes all wrinkled, I suppose we looked like vagabonds from a prisoner of war camp. Just before we boarded the bus, the ambulance driver came in and said, "They told me I'd find you down here. You owe me $10." "Ten dollars?" I asked. "Yes, ten dollars," he repeated. I looked in my billfold and there it was, ten dollars, not a cent more. When I gave that man ten dollars, we were penniless. Once again that put me in a position to trust God and God alone. We were told where our bus was and just as we were getting on the bus a man whom I had never seen before and have never seen since, put some money in my pocket. That fed us till we were home in Los Angeles. As we sat on the bus with tears in our eyes, we were reminded of Psalms 37:25. "*I have been young, and now am old; yet I have not seen the righteous forsaken, nor his seed begging bread.*"

After our arrival in Los Angeles, I went to see the doctor. He said, "Mr. Robertson, your appendix ruptured. Most likely it happened when you crossed the railroad tracks. Somehow, and I don't understand it, a sack was formed around your appendix to keep the poison from going into your system. Your appendix is better protected than it was originally. You will probably never have to worry about it. Don't let anyone disturb that sack. That is what kept you from getting gangrene." I had never heard of such a thing. All that Gunda and I could think to do was to fall on our knees and thank God for his deliverance.

Chapter Seven

Alone

After being in California for several weeks, and having gained some weight and getting some necessary rest, a call came from the Foursquare headquarters. They asked me if I would be willing to go to Pennsylvania and serve as District Superintendent of the Atlantic seaboard. I remembered how God had spoken to me that He was going to call me to a new work and it would be something I had never done before. I instinctively thought, "This is the new call from God for which I have been longing and looking." The funds were so meager that there wasn't enough for the family to go along with me at the time. Gunda was expecting our fourth child, but we both felt this is what I should do. So it was agreed that she would stay in California and I would go to Pennsylvania. When I could save enough money for her to join me, I would send for her and the children. Little did I realize then there would never be enough. Our separation would be for over a year. I want my wife at this point to share that year from her point of view.

"I stayed with Charles' mother. She had an upstairs

apartment far out on Sunset Boulevard. My biggest problems, of course, were the finances and my feeling tired most of the time. Charles would send me what he could as he had to live also. But often that would come to only a few dollars a week.

"When I would take the children with me to do the grocery shopping or for a walk, little Charles would often say, 'Mother, I sure would like to have one of those beautiful apples.' My reply would always have to be, 'Honey, Mommy doesn't have the money today to get it. And you know I would have to buy three of them.' He would look down, but say nothing. Out of the meager allowance I had to be sure I had rice and the basic staples. I also had to be sure I had bread, because the children had to have their lunches when they went to school. We didn't have a refrigerator, only an ice box. I also had to buy ice. It wasn't always easy. Charles was only six years old so I had to take him across Sunset Boulevard; there he would meet his cousin and then they would go on together. It got to the place soon when Brittarose could join him because when she was four and a half, she could start kindergarten. Charles would take her by the hand and they would run hand in hand together to the school. It was about four blocks that they had to go all by themselves. I couldn't go with them because I wasn't feeling well. I had little Darlene; she was still small and wasn't walking as yet. My mother-in-law went to work at six in the morning at the print shop. She would work till ten or eleven at night, so I saw very little of her. The apartment only had three rooms. There was a large living and dining room together, the kitchen and Grandma had the bedroom. There was a let down bed in the living room. All three children and myself slept in that bed. It seemed almost like a nightmare, that whole year. I felt washed out through most of my pregnancy. The children were such good kids, but sometimes, in spite of that, I felt like I was walking up and down the walls. There were times when I became very, very weary and would say, 'Why, Lord?' I never blamed

Charles because he was having a hard time, too. There was nothing else to do; we had put our lives in God's hand and we were not turning back. So we made the best of both situations.

"Once in awhile I would go out and see my mother who now lived in Eagle Rock. When I did that, I had to carry Darlene; Charles would take Brittarose's hand and I would take hold of her other hand. One by one I would lift them on the street car. We had to change cars in downtown Los Angeles then continue for miles to Eagle Rock. When we got off the street car, there was still quite a walk and it was all up hill to my mother's. That was quite a chore but the children were so good and never gave me any trouble.

"All this time Charles was out on the east coast. We wrote back and forth but it was impossible for him to come back and get us because of the finances. He sent me all the money he possibly could. I paid our bills. I bought the food. But there was no money for little toys or trinkets for the kids to play with. What little they had was when we would go to the dime store and buy a coloring book and colors and they would all have to share. At times it seemed impossible, but we got by.

"Then it finally came time for us to have another little baby come into the family. When the little fellow came along, it was during the time when we had the terrible epidemic of flu. At that time my mother had taken pneumonia so I tried to get over and help take care of her. When I did that, the children were left with their aunt for several days. When I came back, the baby had contacted this flu. I couldn't get a doctor at that time. I didn't know what to do, I had always depended on Charles so much in a situation like that. My mother-in-law didn't know what to do either. All of the doctors were so busy at the hospitals they were not making house calls. The baby had developed a problem where he could breathe in but he couldn't breathe out. I had never been around that type of thing at all, and I didn't know what it was. I felt so alone and totally helpless. Finally a doctor did come but he never quite gave me any answers. He said to put Clyde on oxygen, do this and do that but he never came back to see if we were doing it right. I prayed much and did everything that I possibly could. However, Clyde got worse and worse. I finally put him in the hospital. Nothing helped and slowly life left his little body and he was soon back into the arms of Jesus. They said had he lived, that he would have had brain damage. So it was a blessing the Lord took him. But I wondered why it happened; we never could quite figure it all out. On the other hand, my faith spoke and said, 'Lord, You gave him to us for ten weeks and You were good to us. If You felt the need for him, You certainly know what You are doing.' We never were bitter towards the Lord. It did bring Charles home and for that I was both grateful and thankful.''

Gunda never once hinted of the tremendous struggle and anxiety that she was going through. I was so busy that I simply didn't consider all of her hardships and pain. It had become a way of life for both of us. It is hard now when I look back to realize that the money was so scarce. There was no way that I could afford to return when she gave birth to the baby. When I received word that the delivery was fine and that she had given birth to a beautiful, healthy ten pound baby boy, we decided to name him Clyde. There was no reason at all that he should have died. When the word came that he was gone, I was stunned beyond belief. This made me wonder if what I was doing was what the Lord wanted me to do. I decided then and there that I would return home for the funeral of my son and to be with my wife. I flew from Pittsburgh to Kansas City. There I was bumped because of V.I.P. military personnel. That was about 10 o'clock in the evening. From all apparent circumstances, there seemed no way that I would ever get back to Los Angeles in time for my son's funeral. There was a flood in Kansas City. No busses or trains were moving. And to top it off, there were four inches of water on the runway.

Of course my heart and mind were full of questions, why? I had never seen my baby and I wondered if he would fade in and out of my life without his father's eyes ever once looking at him, even in death. The airline gave me no hope at all. However, about three o'clock in the morning they called my name and said they were making up a special flight. I had been chosen to be on it. I gave a sigh of relief and thanked Jesus for getting me on this plane. Little did I realize how significant that prayer was. We were hardly airborne when the pilot came on the intercom and said, "Ladies and gentlemen, I regret to inform you that the plane you were scheduled to depart on at ten p.m. has crashed and there are no survivors."

Instantly my mind thought of Romans 8:28, *"All things work together for good. . ."* I was truly humbled before the Lord, that I even once thought that He was wrong in allowing my trip home to be delayed.

Oh, the joy it was to my heart to hold my precious Gunda in my arms once again. We cried, prayed, cried and did some more praying. For a few moments everything seemed so meaningless.

The children had grown so much that I hardly knew them. It grieved me that I had been gone from them so long. Especially during this very hard time.

After the funeral and when our grief somewhat subsided, I decided to leave the ministry of the Seaboard to be with my wife and family. For the time being I went to work in my Mother's print shop. I had to know now for certain, beyond a shadow of a doubt, what the will of God was for our lives. Gunda and I claimed the verse in Proverbs 3:6, *"In all thy ways acknowledge Him, and He shall direct thy paths."*

Gerald L.K. Smith and myself

Chapter Eight

Gerald L.K. Smith

Mr. and Mrs. Gerald L.K. Smith were soon to become a very intricate part of our lives. Mr. Smith travelled from coast to coast always with his wife, lecturing in every major city in the United States. This was brought on somewhat naturally and inspired by the fact that he had been raised the son, grandson, and great grandson of Christian Church ministers. He had been educated for the ministry and went into it full time constantly lifting up the Lord Jesus Christ. His ministry began in Footville, Wisconsin and he pastored various churches including the University Christian Church in Indianapolis, Indiana. Later the Kingshighway Christian Church in Shreveport, Louisiana.

His great dedication and consecration to Jesus Christ and the United States of America threw him into the public eye. As pastor of the leading church of the Christian denomination, he was constantly called on for various civic duties, one of which was dedicating the United States Air Force base in Bosier City, Louisiana. Moments before he was to offer the prayer of dedication, the Colonel stepped up beside him and said, "Mr. Smith, don't use the name of Christ; we don't use His name when we make government dedications. Just use the name God." Mr. Smith turned to him quite abruptly and said, "I don't know how to pray if I don't pray in the name of the Lord Jesus Christ." As he prayed the prayer of dedication it was without question in the name of the Lord Jesus Christ. It was that type of thing that brought the wrath and fire of government officials down on him. Just doing what Christ expects a Christian to do. I had heard Mr. Smith on radio many times and I had read many of his writings. When I heard that he was going to hold meetings in the Los Angeles area, of course I wanted to attend, which I did. We were already doing much of his printing in my mother's print shop and because of those meetings with Mr. Smith we began doing even more. It wasn't long until he hired me, part time, and I was sitting on the platform with him.

Many of the meetings that we held were picketed. At some, there were even riots that started. At one such meeting, the mayor of Los Angeles was knocked down and beaten. It wasn't long until I knew what the plague of communism was and the message Mr. Smith was giving. The Communist aim was to take over America and that's all there was to it. His message also was "Christ first in America." He often said, "People, we must protect the Constitution and preserve our Christian heritage." It seemed wherever he went he was opposed, not because of what he was going to say, but because of the potential of his leadership. Many of the men who were in control of the elected officials didn't want anyone to come on the scene who wouldn't bow to their dictates. Mr Smith showed absolute promise of thinking for himself. He had charisma and a great message. People flocked to him to hear what he had to say.

Many of the country's senators and congressmen sought his counsel and listened to what he had to say. But they were somewhat like Nicodemus who came to Jesus by night. They'd slip in and out to see him. They highly respected him but were frightened to be seen with him. It wasn't long until I thought Gerald L.K. Smith was one of the greatest men I had ever met. And I knew he had one of the greatest messages. He was a vibrant Christian, not the sloppy sanctimonious kind, but a straight forward one. He carried himself well and kept his wife with him constantly. He was appropriately never out of her sight. That was demonstrated a few years later when we had the privilege of being in Colonel Beatty's home. At that time he was head of the military intelligence during the second World War. One of his assignments was to keep twenty-four hour watch on Mr. Smith and, as a result, assigned many men to watch him. Every two weeks he would change these men. I'll never forget when Colonel Beatty turned to Mrs. Smith and said, "Mrs. Smith, there's one thing I can tell you about your husband. I know every individual he has met with, and spoken with. I know every conversation that he ever had and I can tell you in absoluteness that there has never been another woman in your husband's life." She quietly turned to Colonel Beatty and said, "Thank you, Colonel, but the Lord has also shown me that."

During the depression, while Mr. Smith was in Shreveport, Louisiana, there was a period of time when thousands of people who only owed several hundred dollars on their homes before the mortgages would be paid off were having their mortgages foreclosed on them. Mr. Smith, realizing the unfairness and depravity of the situation, called Governor Hughey Long and asked the Governor if there wasn't something that could be done for these poor people. "It's not right for these people to be losing everything. They have been faithful so long and they owe so little. Please, can't we do something for these people?" "You're right, Dr. Smith. Stay right by the phone and I'll call you back in a few minutes," said the governor. In less than thirty minutes he called Mr. Smith back and said, "You call so and so and tell him what to do because, Dr. Smith, I've told him that whatever you tell him to do he must do it!" He called the bank commissioner. Something was worked out and a plan was devised to save these mortgage loans just in the State of Louisiana. As I stated before, Mr. Smith was pastoring in Shreveport's Kingshighway Christian Church. Well, it wasn't long till he discovered that he had bankers on his board. They rose up and threatened to throw him out of the church for meddling in their monetary business. As a result, he resigned the church and took his stand for America and her people. Through his efforts nobody else in Louisiana lost their homes. They were given a chance to hold on till the federal law came into effect the following July. That was his introduction to Hughey Long. This moved him from the pulpit to the radio and to the public meeting hall, where he proclaimed the constitution of the United States and the Christian tradition of this great land. Immediately he stirred the animosity not only of the bankers but of the anti-christ. One might say that he spent the next period of his life defending the constitution and our Christian Heritage.

Having travelled the land from North to South and East to West crisscrossing it many times, Mr. Smith became very much aware of the fact that the communists were out to destroy America. The fellowship between Mr. Smith and Hughey Long increased and it wasn't long until Governor Long became the U.S. Senator from Louisiana. There was a time when Mr. Smith along with Townsend and Father Coughland, joined together to elect a man president of the United States. They selected Hughey P. Long as the candidate. Before the convention could be held, Long was assassinated. Even though a dictaphone recording of secret meetings that were held discussing Huey Long's assassination were put into the congressional record a month before his assassination, nothing was done about it. It was carried out very much as it was predicated it would be. This caused Mr. Smith to become absolutely serious about protecting the Constitutional rights of the United States. He himself turned down a request to become the Republican candidate for the Presidency because he felt the President could not be free but only a pawn to those who would surround him. He realized as far back as the late 30's that there were evil forces trying to take over the United States. At that time, even though America was coming through and surviving the depression, he saw that the depression was manipulated much as our petroleum crises have been in recent years. The forces of the anti-christ were building, building, and building their cause. His last sermon on the radio was *"Christ First in America."* It was after that message that Franklin Roosevelt ordered Smith taken off the air, all over the United States. He thought that he was secure in that he had a $27,000 contract on a strong Mexican radio station that beamed far into the United States, but even there he lost his program. The State Department had him cancelled from the Mexican station. So his stand for God and country had been thrown into the political arena. He was never allowed back on the air again.

He discovered that the same people who were controlling politics were also at the same time infiltrating and manipulating the various counsels of churches. It was shocking to realize the wide-spread powers of corruption and communism even in the church.

One time I was in New York City and was in the office of the anti-defamation league. While I was there, the telephone rang and it was Congressman Hayes from Arkansas. He stated, "I'm in Florida carrying out your wishes, but if you don't get me out of here and back in Arkansas, I'm going to lose the election." Gilbert said to him, "You've got to stay in Florida, you've got to campaign for my man down there. We'll send someone into Arkansas to do your campaigning." As a result, Hayes lost the election. However, later he was elected to the presidency of the Southern Baptist Convention. It became apparent that he was doing the will of the anti-defamation league rather than working for himself. He was doing as they wished and when you defy Mr. Big, you are in trouble.

We began holding meetings talking on the subject of prayer in America and specifically in schools. This was in the 50's long before the Supreme Court made their diabolical ruling banning prayer from the classroom. Mr. Smith announced that I would open the meeting in prayer. Well, that opened the floodgates, at least against me. I was called, my mother was called, and both of us were threatened and told that if I attended that meeting I would be killed. I had hundreds of calls and threats concerning that meeting in one of Hollywood, California's larger high schools. Of course that merely set me off. Whenever I'm told I can't do something, that makes me more determined than ever. I attended that meeting and opened in prayer in spite of everything. The crowds that night were tremendous. The high school auditorium was packed and hundreds had to be turned away. Mr. Smith preached a sermon on the fall of America and how that all that was Christian was going to be virtually outlawed or suspended or taken through the courts and the church would finally be squeezed and squeezed until it had virtually no effect. This was going to be done to a Christian nation. It's awful to think prayer has been eliminated from the school system when one of our text books used to be the Word of God.

At this point I was still working for Mr. Smith part time. I was also working for my mother in the print shop. It was that meeting that really put me into the full time work with him. By now I knew him well enough that I knew that when I joined him full time, I was jumping into the lion's den. But I knew that that was but a stepping stone to the calling that God had been waiting to do in my life. Gunda was 100% behind me; she was all for my alliance with Mr. Smith for we both knew that his first alliance was serving Jesus Christ. My mother had been printing all his material so she knew where he stood. Gunda, my mother and I decided the Word of God told us that if we submitted to God, resisted the devil, he would flee from us. We were readily reminded how God had rid our home of the bedbugs and rats. Now the Lord showed us that He would take care of us and protect us not only from those pestilences, but from people as well.

Travelling with Mr. Smith and being associated with him opened many doors for me with senators, congressmen and governors. I remember as if it were only yesterday meeting with one of the governors of the South. That was the day of the Dixiecrats. I had an appointment, but for some reason unknown to me the secretary came and said, "There will be about an hour's delay in your appointment with the governor. Mr. Robertson, they have just hung this old chandelier here in the mansion; it had been hid during the Civil War. I have hundreds of crystals here to hang on it. Rather than you just sitting there waiting, why don't you help me put these crystals on the chandelier." So I climbed up the rickety ladder and there I consumed that hour placing crystals on that beautiful Pre-Civil War chandelier. So I feel to this day that I had a little part in the history of Mississippi.

I found myself in Washington, D.C. many times. For the most part, the senators and congressmen were very cordial. One day after a disgruntled Puerto Rican shot up the Congress, I went in and was going to find a seat in the balcony. A policeman came to me and said, "Sir, stop. You can't go in there." Before I had a chance to even say, "Why not?", one of the heads of security spoke up for me and said, "I'll speak for this man. I know who he is. This is Charles Robertson; he works for Gerald L.K. Smith." With that, my recommendation was completed and I was ushered to one of the front row seats of the balcony. Mr. Smith was highly respected because he always spoke the truth and he never intentionally said anything to hurt anybody. He simply told it as it was. There is the old saying, "The hit dog always yelps." We'd also find ourselves in the United Nations and he'd go from one office to the other. While he was visiting, I could also visit. Most people never got past the lounge.

There had been an incident where a school teacher was thrown out of the second story window of the Russian Embassy in New York. I was asking some questions. I thought I might have some information to add to the investigation for our magazine as to why the school teacher of Denmark was killed. I was sent to the suite of the United Nation's legation from Denmark and there I was presented to Count Mulkey. We got into quite a discussion on communism. In the midst of this conversation he opened up his desk and pulled out the magazine, *The Cross and The Flag*. He said, "Mr. Robertson, you need to know this man Mr. Smith." I said, "Yes sir, I fully agree with you. I already know this man." At that I pulled out the next issue of *The Cross and The Flag* and showed him. "Mr. Robertson," he queried, "Could you arrange a meeting with Mr. Smith and myself?" I said, "Certainly, may I use your phone?" At that I picked up the phone and called the Plaza Hotel and asked Mr. Smith if I could bring Count Mulkey from Denmark over. His reply was of course, "Certainly." I turned to the ambassador and said, "I don't have a car here, we'll have to take a cab." "Don't worry about that, Mr. Robertson," he said, "I have a car." He made a call and had his car brought around to the front of the United Nations building. I was amazed when we went out the door and there sat this beautiful $26,000 Bently Limousine. (Today its value would be three times that amount.) "Mr. Robertson, you get in the front seat by the driver," the Count said. Then he went around to the other side of the car and said to the chauffeur, "I'm going to drive today." At that the chauffeur got out and the ambassador got in the driver's seat and away we went to the Plaza Hotel. He met with Mr. and Mrs. Smith and that was the beginning of many such meetings. One point that he did make during the conversation in regard to our publication was, "Mr. Smith, if some of the other publications that I have been

78

reading would have had your investigators, they could publish material such as you have done. Your intelligence has proven better than Scotland Yard and the F.B.I." Mr. Smith replied, "We have Charles to thank for that." I felt very complimented.

Several visits later the Count said to me, "Mr. Robertson, someday I want to introduce you to the head of the United Nations intelligence. I think you could teach him some things." For some reason I never kept that commitment, but it was a high compliment. I knew that God had brought me a long way from the copperheads and blue racers of Kentucky. Actually in reality not very far, for there in Kentucky I served the Lord of Lords and King of Kings, and I was still serving the same Master, the Lord Jesus Christ.

Because I wanted to keep a clear testimony at the United Nations, I learned to drink a lot of tomato juice. It seemed as though at the United Nations whenever you met someone, you had to have a drink. I would not drink alcoholic beverages, so tomato juice was my answer. One day I was complimented by one of the Arab representatives who said to me, "Charles, you're a better Moslem than we are because you don't partake of these things." Because they trusted me, I had the privilege of meeting at that time Pasha Assum, the head of the Muslim faith. He came to America at this particular time expecting to have dialogue with various Christians and to find out the true meaning of Christianity. It was his desire at that time to accept Christ as the Messiah of the Muslim faith. But when he came to New York, it seemed that every one he met was a non-believer or a compromising Christian. He was totally disillusioned. I look back now on that moment of history and have thought many times how the course of events could have been changed if he could have met real Christians. The Muslim religion could have accepted Jesus Christ as their Messiah. We never know how we influence people who are watching us. I'm afraid that all too often people of other faiths cannot understand what has happened to

America. I feel this is the day that we need to make our faith keen and our conviction strong. We need to exert ourselves to the point of tearing down the strongholds of Satan in our nation before it is too late.

About this time our last child Kay came into the world right along with the atomic bomb and she was introduced along with atomic energy. Believe me when I say that to this day she exudes energy like that bomb as she walks with Jesus.

Our children, Chuck, Brittarose,
Darlene and Kay

Myself, Mr. & Mrs. Gerald L.K. Smith

Gunda, myself and Mrs. Elna M. Smith

Our Glendale home

Gunda in front of Glendale home

Chapter Nine

God Bless America

While I was working with Mr. Smith roaming over the countryside and meeting all these celebrities, our children were now in their teens and were all working for Mr. Smith. They were growing up so fast that I hardly knew them. It was such a demanding job I had with Mr. Smith that I was still away from home weeks on ends. The Smiths did not always have a beautiful home in which to live. As late as 1947 everything they possessed was in the trunk of their car. They went from hotel to hotel, rented apartment to rented apartment. They had no bank account. As the money came in, they used all of it for the meetings and lectures. There was a time when they had to mortgage their car to pay the salary of the office force.

I can remember Mrs. Smith's saying that when they had been in New York several years and had been laboring in trying to teach the people what Communism was, they came to a day when they were down to their last penny. She was in the hotel and Mr. Smith had gone out to get some cottage cheese and a couple of items that they could eat in the hotel room. Suddenly an angel appeared to Mrs. Smith and said, "Mrs. Smith, everything is going to be all right. You will be taken care of, don't you worry about these things, for you are doing the work of the Lord." That very day they received a special delivery letter from Pennsylvania with $100.00 in it. Every week from that day for several years they would receive this anonymous $100.00. That was the backbone of finances that carried them through. God always provided. There was never an abundance but there was always sufficient. No matter what program or what effort he would put forth, the needs were always met.

When he was in Denver, Colorado on a speaking engagement someone put arsenic in his coffee and poisoned him. They were living in Tulsa, so Mrs. Smith took him back to Tulsa as soon as she could. The doctors, not only in Colorado, but in Tulsa, said that he had arsenic poisoning. He was fortunate that it was not a lethal dose. However, a few grains more would have killed him. They warned him to be very careful where he ate and what he ate and who he was around because arsenic stays in the body's system.

It was then that they decided that they had to begin to think about settling down somewhere. Although they were in a rented home, they looked around and found a beautiful brick structure that could be had for a very small down payment. For years they made payments on that house which was later sold to be used in the construction of *The Great Passion Play*.

Gunda and I had learned how to put the pennies and nickels together and make them count. My salary was still very small, but God and Gunda seemed to make every dollar stretch to three. God had given us good lessons prior to this time. We had moved several times. Each time progressing in our home. Our last move in California was to Glendale. Mr. and Mrs. Smith were living in Los Felis by the entrance to Griffith Park. We could look across the valley from our home and see theirs. We were just minutes away from one another but yet a valley apart. I could respond, or any of us, to any emergency quickly. I was working now for him full time. The Print Shop was doing most of the printing for Mr. Smith. The magazine, *The Cross and The Flag,* was being printed elsewhere. We now had four Davidson off-set presses and we would handle most of the printing and the mailing of all of the various literature. After the printing was done, we would call volunteers to the Embassy Auditorium, which we used to do our mailing. At times there would be fifty to eighty volunteers to handle the surge of mail. This was done every week or sometimes twice a week depending on the amount of mail. We took all of our printing down to the Embassy and there we would stamp, address and stuff the envelopes, preparing them for mailing. I enjoyed so much the times when I would work with these volunteers. They were from the very young to the very old. Most were senior citizens, but very active and very vital to the work of Mr. Smith. Many times we would put out over 200,000 pieces in one day. The volunteers would bring their sack lunches and they ate whenever they felt like it, because everything was volunteer, but believe me they worked harder than any paid employee would ever work.

The mailings went all over the world but basically in the United States. From these mailings we could set up meetings in various communities and they were also the major source of our funding.

In the early days the organization was a national political party, so reports had to be sent in to the government at least five times a year.

There was a period in the early fifties when it was almost impossible for a third party to get on the voting ballots. So Mr. Smith asked me if I would lend my name to serve on the ballot as his vice-president, as he, at that time, was running for president. We were totally amazed at how many votes we got. We were on the ballot in twenty-three states. This was done basically for legal purposes, to show the impossibility of a third party candidate getting on the ballot in many of the states. For example: in California, you could not get on the ballot for less than three million dollars in charges. I think when Wallace got on the ballot there, it cost him six million, just for the state of California. When you do that across the nation, it is easy to see how one could spend two hundred million dollars. It is so out of proportion that it takes a man's initiative away from him and makes him the puppet of a group. Thus not allowing his true leadership to flourish, as we can see in Washington this very day.

Between the Congress and the advisors to the President, an elected leader, he doesn't have much of a free hand.

Our cause was written up by most of the legal publications. They lauded our efforts because it was done in such a way that it made a point and personalities were lost in the issue. The issue was the big thing and a lot of forums were opened up to us as a result. But believe me so was the persecution, the telephone threats, and the mail threats. For instance: one morning our telephone rang and it was my insurance broker. He said, "Mr. Robertson, I am sorry, but today we are canceling your insurance because of the activity in which you are involved."

I not only could not get life insurance, I could not get car or home insurance. I had become too much of a risk. Jesus was our only source. This little poem says it all.

> He is ahead of you — as your Shepherd
> He is behind you — as your Rearguard
> He is above you — as your Covering
> He is beneath you — as your Foundation
> He is beside you — as your Friend
> He is within you — as your Life

We had gone to San Francisco, as we had for many years, on the founding anniversary of the United Nations. While we were there the chief of detectives came to me and said, "Charles, Mr. Smith was here last year and he held meetings on the steps of the Memorial Auditorium. We were able to get many pictures of the radicals and were able to indentify many of them. We were wondering if you would be so kind as to do this again. We will surround the auditorium with police and put patrol cars on every block. We will do our very best to quarantee your safety. We would like to get more pictures and be able to identify more people that are in subversive ranks. I cannot think of any occasion that would get us a better time and a better selection of these people."

We didn't hold an outdoor meeting but we did have one inside and the police took their photographs. The entire situation was very dangerous because of various unions and at that time they were a very radical bunch. Walter Reuther's brother had written him from Moscow saying, "Keep on for Soviet America." They had tried to get communism in the unions and were successful. We all know it only takes a little handful of corrupt men to filter to the top to ruin great organizations.

In San Francisco we held some of our finest meetings, especially on the tenth and twentieth anniversaries of the United Nations. It was at these meetings that Mr. Smith informed America that the United Nations was basically a Communist front.

One of the interesting things that few know about the United Nations headquarters is that when you step on the grounds, you are no longer on American soil. You are no longer under American protection. You are on foreign soil under complete control of the United Nations, no matter if you are a visitor or an ambassador. When you enter those grounds, you are subject to their laws, their justice, and their protection, whatever it might be. As you walk into the lobby of the United Nations, the first thing you will see are the big, beautiful doors and on the doors are all the mythological characters one could imagine. Inside is the huge statue of Zeus, the mythological god. There is no room in the

United Nations for Jesus Christ. You are an unknown character whenever you go into that building believing in Christ. As you enter into the United Nations building, you will find murals depicting how man rose out of the filth of the world and has ascended up to the point where he is ready for Utopia. All of these depict the total accomplishment of man with God playing no part in his destiny whatsoever. This is atheistic humanism personified. One of the early secretary generals was quoted as saying, "The problem with the world today is that there are too many Christians. If there were no Christians, the world could have peace."

Most of us think that the United Nations was organized so that man could talk his problems out and save mankind from the holocaust of war. In reality, I believe, the United Nations was created to establish war between man and God. Then man without God could control the world and thus make a platform for the anti-christ. The vast majority of members of the United Nations are not Christians. They are atheists or false god worshipers. So we have within the confines of our own nation a festering cancer of anti-christ. This should have never been allowed to be brought on the shores of the United States of America.

The United Nations is an outgrowth of the League of Nations which was set up to bring world peace, but it failed. One can only wonder if the League of Nations wasn't the first beast because it had no power. The United Nations has power. If you will look at the voting, for the most part you will find that the United States has only two or three nations that vote with us. The United Nations has its own troops and its own voice. There are executive orders where the American armed forces can be turned over to the United Nations.

There are certainly things that we as concerned Christians need to look into, observe, and understand. Oftentimes we only see the superficial but never get down to the heart of the matter even as Jesus Christ Himself said, *"They honor me with their lips but their hearts are far from me.*" The scripture also tells us that men look at the outward but God alone can know the heart. That was what Mr. Smith and I tried to bring to the attention of the public and were nearly killed for doing so.

I believe that's why there are so many radicals and extremists and hijackers in the world today. They realize that the way to bring attention to their cause is to do something criminal and they will get world wide attention. For example, the recent TWA hijacking in Lebanon. For days the world's eyes were on those few men. Yes, it was tragic for those lives to be in peril and to lose the life of that one young man, but look at how many tens of thousands of people are being slaughtered every day in Russia, Afghanistan, Vietnam, Cambodia, China, Africa, and it never makes the newspapers let alone television. We've got to be very careful how we allow the publicity to go forth with such power and magnitude over a hijacked plane.

Most of the time I served as a front man for Mr. and Mrs. Smith. I would make their appointments and make the arrangements necessary for his speaking engagements. While I was in New York, it came my lot to call on Kin Saud of Saudia, Arabia. We'd had a very profitable meeting with him and then were his honored guests at a gala reception that he held in New York. We were very fortunate to be his guest.

During the time of Nasser of Egypt, I called on the Egyptian legation. They had sent a representative from Nasser to talk to Mr. Smith. Mr. Smith outlined to them was was going to happen. He said to the Egyptians, "Now that you're building the Aswan Dam you are going to need more support to pay for it. I believe the American Government is going to pull the rug out from under you and you're going to have to turn to somebody else for help. The only one who is probably going to help you will be Russia. The purpose they will have for helping you will be to get their military into Egypt. They are going to want to control Egypt." He continued to outline the whole scenario. History does record that America did withdraw their money from the Aswan Dam project. Egypt did turn to Russia and they brought in all kinds of advisers. We know that they numbered into the thousands. Nasser kept a strong hand on things and was not ready to give Egypt, at any cost, to Russia. As a result he was killed.

When Sadat came into power, he expelled all of the Russians and that led to his demise. So far, Egypt has been able to stay out of their clutches but the whole Middle Eastern conflict is going to keep building and keep building until catastrophe strikes. There will be a time when the Lord will take over and He will rule and reign. But Satan's ambition is to get there first. Set it up as his kingdom and rule from Jerusalem in the place of Christ. That's when the big conflict will come. Right now we're moving into that period, regardless of how we look at it with our personal theology. One may explain it one way and another, but we all know that we're getting down to the zero hour when something is going to happen.

I had the privilege of doing much of the research work on various programs for Mr. Smith. Once a man came to me and showed me photos that he had gotten out of Russia. I didn't know what to do with them. I tried to get a Congressional Committee to listen to me, but no one would listen. Finally, I did arrange a meeting for him with one of the representatives of the Congressional Committee. Mr. Smith, fortunately, was able to convey to him the importance of the photographs. When the investigation was finally done by our government, they discovered those photographs were underground markings for submarines to come along the east coast of America. From there they could aim their missiles on any target in the United States. I don't know how the man ever came into the possession of those photos, but when they were turned over to the proper authorities, they were certainly used. Those markers were removed.

One of the greatest men that I met while I was travelling with Mr. Smith and in my many visits to Washington, D.C., was Senator Jenner from the state of Illinois. I will never forget when he came to the point in his life where he felt he could no longer stay in Washington.

He turned to me and said, "Mr. Robertson, Washington is destroying my home, and my family. Therefore, I do not believe I am going to seek re-election. It has gotten so bad here, there are perhaps only five free votes in all of Congress." Now that's pretty bad when a congressman or senator cannot vote as he pleases and he must be manipulated either by money, blackmail or political pressure. We wonder why our nation isn't a great nation, as it used to be. I believe it is because we do not have free leaders. Leaders who really can stand up and say that this is what America stands for!

I said, "Senator Jenner, what are you going to do if some of these things you fear, happen to this country?"

"Well," he said, "I've already bought a farm down in the Ozarks. I'm going there and disappear."

"Why," I chuckled, "You're too well known to disappear."

"You might think so," he said, "But I've got another name I'll be using down there."

That made me ponder how many important people are hiding out afraid of what's coming upon the world, instead of standing up and trying to do something about it. We read in the Scriptures that we are supposed to tear down the strongholds of Satan. Christians need to band together and forget some of their petty problems and their peripheral doctrines and become a one-voice-force in America. God help us if we don't!

Penn Castle

Emmet Sullivan and myself where
Mr. Smith made the "X"

Chapter Ten

The Statue

While I was visiting Eureka Springs with the Smiths, Mr. Smith said, "Charles, the farms are disappearing and the American way of life as we know it now will soon be gone. If we don't do something soon to establish something here our ancestors are not going to know what the Ozark farm or this way of life is like. We need to get a log cabin and restore it, set up a little early American farm so the children can come and look at it. They need to know how the people worked so hard to establish this country and develop it."

When Mr. Smith spoke, I moved. I called several realtors and not one of them was able to come up with anything. I told them to keep looking. We had returned to the west coast when I received a telephone call from Tilman Morgan and he said, "Charles, I haven't found the log cabin, but there is a stone mansion that certainly needs some tender loving care and an owner that could restore it. It contains fourteen rooms, built out of hand cut rock." He told me the selling price. My only reply was, "Well, Tilman, I'll have to tell Mr. and Mrs. Smith and see what they think." I told them about it and much to my amazement he said, "Charles, you and Gunda haven't had a vacation together for some time. I think you should take her and go back to Eureka Springs, Arkansas and see about that house."

So we drove back to Eureka Springs and for the first time saw Penn Castle. I had a very strange urging from the Spirit about the place and looked at my wife and said, "Honey, we've got to take pictures of this. There is no way I could go back and describe this to the Smiths. I don't want them to be influenced in any way by what I think or how I speak or because of my own personal feelings."

We took pictures and went back to Tulsa. After we were there for a day or so, we decided to go back and take some more pictures. So we returned to Eureka Springs and took several more rolls of photographs. We sent these back to Los Angeles, so by the time we returned, the photos would be waiting for us. The following day after our return I took the pictures and showed them to Mr. and Mrs. Smith. They flipped through three or four and Mr. Smith said, "Charles, I sense there's something about this and you're not telling me the whole story. Now tell me."

"Mr. Smith, there's something that I feel, nothing more than that," I responded. At that Mr. Smith said, "Charles, I want to buy it. Go and call your real estate agent and tell him we'll pay one half of whatever they're asking." I looked at him somewhat puzzled and perplexed, but I did just what he said.

I called the real estate agent and said, "Tilman, we want to buy that house. We'll pay them one half of what they are asking." On the other end I could hear laughter, almost a cynical laughter, and then he said, "Why Charles, I wouldn't insult my clients like that." "Now wait a minute, Tilman," I said, "You told me to come back, talk to Mr. Smith and make you an offer. Now I'm doing that. We will pay one half of what they are asking. Now please relay that to the owners." "All right,

Charles, I'll do it, but I certainly hope you are not expecting a favorable answer," Tilman replied. In about three days Tilman called and told us the owners had signed their acceptance. The Smiths flew to Eureka Springs and signed the papers. They bought Penn Castle sight unseen except for the photographs that Gunda and I had taken. This was the first stepping stone.

John Frank from Frankoma Pottery was a very close friend of the Smiths. One day he was in Eureka visiting and he asked Mr. Smith, "If you find a hill top around here with a spring on it, I'd like to buy it for an investment." "Sure, John. I'll have Charles see what he can find," Mr. Smith answered. Now I was out searching for property again but this time not for the Smiths but for John Frank. I talked to Norman Tucker and in a couple of days he called and said, "Charles, if you will tell Mr. Smith to step out in front of Penn Castle and look across the valley, he'll see three mountain tops that have been cleared off. Tomatoes were grown there last year and now I have the right to sell this property."

When I told them this, Mr. and Mrs. Smith and myself stood on the lawn in front of Penn Castle and I pointed out the three mountain tops. I saw a gleam come into their eyes. Slowly Mr. Smith said, "Charles, get Mr. Tucker on the phone. I want to go up there and see that property." So the three of us along with Mr. Tucker ascended up an old wagon road to the top of what is now called Magnetic Mountain. As we stood there, an awesome look came over Mr. Smith's face as he spoke to his wife Elna, "Honey, this is what I've been looking for." "Yes, Gerald," was his wife's reply. "This is where we should build the monument to the Lord."

They had been looking on the west coast, the Rockies, the Appalachians, all over the United States to fulfill their vision but had found nothing. It was either too high or too inaccessible or it just simply didn't feel right. As we stood there, I sensed in my spirit that this was indeed a momentous occasion. Slowly they walked together over to a particular spot on that mountain top. He took his foot and there he marked an "X". "Charles, this is where we are going to erect that seven story statue of Jesus Christ, the monument to my Saviour that I've always wanted to build." I stood there awe struck. I knew he had wanted to build a monument but I certainly didn't realize it was going to be seven stories tall.

After a few moments of absolute silence, he once again began to speak, "Charles, there is no board that is going to press me to accomplish this. Therefore, I want to go immediately and give a release to the newspapers and tell them that the Christ of the Ozarks statue is going to be placed on this mountain. Because of that publicity I know I'll keep my promise to the public and they will make me follow through." Still somewhat stunned, I made no reply. We went immediately to the realtor, signed the papers, paid for the property, and went down to the newspaper office and made the release. I remember well the time John Frank visited us. Mr. Frank asked me if I would deliver a message to Mr. Smith. "Charles, tell Mr. Smith not to build the statue. It will be a failure, a mockery, and it will break his heart." I stood there somewhat astonished, but I did promise to take that message to Mr. Smith. Mr. Smith simply replied, "Charles, I don't believe God would ask me to do something that would end in failure."

Of course the results can be seen today. Young and old, people of every nationality, can come and view the statue and immediately recognize some attribute or characteristic or be inspired by the artistic work that was accomplished by the hands of Emmet Sullivan the sculptor, and his co-workers.

As the sun moves and the clouds form and pass over, and the light changes the characteristics of the statue, it is my belief that many people see not the figure made of mortar, but a reflection of their own lives. For some will stand before the statue and say, "Look, look how stern his facial expression is." Another standing six feet from that person will say, "I've never seen such compassion, and such love on a face." One time a girl standing at the statue asked her mother if she could touch it. Her mother said, "No, you can't touch, don't you see that chain that's around the statue to keep people back?" The girl was persistent and finally persuaded her mother to let her slip under the chain and touch the statue of Christ. Upon touching it the child said, "Oh! Mama! Jesus is so big, He's so big."

That made me once again realize that our God is truly big and truly great. He is not inanimate as our statue, but He is a living God mindful of each and every one of us. He is compassionate, tender, loving and kind. As this age comes to a close, how thankful we can be that God sent His Son as a little babe who grew into manhood that He might be the Lamb slain from the foundation of the world. The atonement for all of our sins. When He comes again, He will be coming as the Lord of Lords and the King of Kings and then the day of mercy will be over. It behooves each and every one of us to have our faith in Christ and to have committed our lives to Him before He comes.

When they come or when they see the statue from the valley of the city, they are reminded there is a God. We've had many different reactions of people as they've visited through the years. One man wrote on the card and said, "I'm an atheist and this is the first time I've ever felt there was actually a God."

Another man had put twenty years in the navy and when he came home, he had no time for God. He and his mother were visiting Eureka Springs and driving up Spring Street. She was even afraid to mention church to her son. He looked across the valley and saw the statue. He pulled the car to the curb, stopped and said, "Mother, I've got to re-commit my life to Jesus Christ and I've got to do it right now."

Jesus said, *"And I, if I be lifted up from the earth, will draw all men unto me. John 12:32."*

The Christ of the Ozarks

Gunda and myself at dedication of
The Christ of the Ozarks Statue

Chapter Eleven

Eureka Springs

Mr. and Mrs. Smith almost every spring and fall went to a small town in northwest Arkansas nestled in the hills to relax and to be refreshed. Their legal residence was Tulsa, Oklahoma. They spent about half of the year on the west coast and the rest of the time at their residence in Tulsa when he wasn't travelling. Mrs. Smith wrote the following comments on Eureka Springs:

EUREKA SPRINGS, GEM OF THE OZARKS

"Anyone who has not seen Eureka and her immediate environment has not seen the Ozarks. The apex of beauty and intrigue, as far as the Ozarks is concerned, is reached within the Eureka Circle which is scarcely more than twenty-five miles in diameter.

"Who can describe Eureka Springs? This quaint, inspiring, sophisticated, little city cannot be described, it can only be experienced. I lack the expert vocabulary in which to describe its flowers, and its rolling hills. One would require a post-graduate course in ornithology in order to appreciate in the fullest intelligence the bird life of this beforested community.

"I make no pretense at summarizing all the assets of this shangrila of beauty but there is one way that I can speak with authority — I can summarize the impression and the effects that moved my heart and caused me to fall in love with Eureka Springs enough to restore an old beautiful home (Penn Castle) and live in the satisfaction that in this the day of the destroyers who are demolishing beauty in the name of progress, I was able to do one little thing in the preservation of traditional charm. Forgive me if I number my points:

"1. The people — Strangers are impressed immediately with the cordiality, the friendliness, and the wholesome radiation of personality manifest in Eureka Springs. People coming here expecting to find a community dominated by ignorance and provincialism experience a beautiful feeling in the atmosphere of intelligence, culture, and sophistication. At the same time, the community is blessed by the richness of pioneer stock, native sons, and bloodline personalities which reach back through the centuries.

"2. Civic pride — No intelligent observer can walk through the streets of Eureka without knowing that civic pride prevails. A hundred symptoms reveal that somewhere a little handful of civic leaders are burning the midnight oil to figure out ways and means to increase the charm and usability of this historic community.

"3. The mountains — Unless one has driven into Eureka Springs, he has not seen the mountains. Every turn in the road, every bend in the street, every glimpse of a new angle brings a thrilling surprise to the visitor. These mountains have not been organized. They rise like giant hand-made muffins clothed with green, gold, silver, and auburn. In the fall the color of these mountains and the trees framed and outlined by the winding roads, trails, and paths make the words "riot of color" seem like a weak expression. Artists tell me that when the colors are reproduced accurately, outside connoisseurs who have never seen the Eureka Ozarks, insist that the realistic artist, no matter how accurate he is, has exaggerated the vividness of the color.

"4. Water — Bubbling springs have broken out by the scores throughout the entire area with nearly three score springs within the boundaries of the little city. The water is not only sweet, cold, and tasty, but it has a purity and therapeutic quality for drinking and bathing. Eureka is indeed a center that might well be referred to as having the "water of life."

"5. I have friends who have made expensive journeys to Europe in order that they might seek out a quaint little village in Bavaria or Italy or France where they could "Ooh and ah" but when they had found their village and "ooh'd and ah'd", they had not found anything as beautiful as Eureka Springs. Those who live here year in and year out and are faced with some of the practical responsibilities of maintaining this beautiful community may grow a bit impatient with some of its antiquities; but, I say, from the bottom of my heart, of the construction of Eureka and its relation to the topography of the area, that each and every part of it radiates beauty. I think of one spot where an old chimney still stands alone. Artists travel hundreds of miles to paint pictures of sights less aesthetic. I see beauty in vacant lots where degenerated houses have left well constructed retainer walls, built of native stone, laid so straight and so perfectly that even without mortar the walls have remained solid and firm. The word for that sort of stone construction is "dry stone."

"6. A four-story community — I thrilled to the very center of my heart when I first caught the view on Spring Street of Perkins Lumber Yard on story one, the library on story two, the Catholic Church on story three, and the Crescent Hotel on story four. Stacked in an exotic and aesthetic beauty that no modern architect could reproduce. There are enough angles and scenes and views to challenge the talent of ten-thousand photographers and all the great artists that live. Recently, I had a guest and he vowed that he was going out to take candid shots of every sensational and inspiring scene that he could find. Hours and hours later he returned to report that he had taken over seventy-five shots and hadn't even gotten a good start. "Furthermore," he said, "These seventy-five shots are the sort of thing that I could find no place else." This man was not only a professional but has been associated with one of the most important photographic organizations in America.

"7. The stone walls — No modernistic nut and no lunatic, sailing under the banner of progress, could destroy the stone wall construction of this town with even bulldozers and atom bombs. One thing that makes Eureka so choice and intriguing and quaint and super beautiful is the fact that its antiquity is beyond the destructive reach of those who love to ridicule tradition, time, and antique charm.

"8. The hotels — There is nothing in America that can duplicate the Crescent Hotel and the Basin Park Hotel. One could hope that a magic wand of generous expenditure could restore both of these magnificent structures to the original lushness of the first builders. Discerning observers often pay tribute to the Nichols Family and to the Fuller Family who have held these forts of beauty. They give to the Americans a classic touch of tradition which can scarcely be duplicated anywhere else in the U.S.A."

When we came to Eureka Springs it was almost a Ghost Town. There were no gift shops and only very few stores were open. There was a barber shop, five and dime, drug store and the two hotels. However, when we did stay at one of the hotels, it was like being in the desert all alone. Most of the time there would only be one or two guests. The area was more depressed at the time than the Appalachian mountain area. Land and houses were being sold at rock bottom prices. The yearly income of the average family around the country was only $900.

You could buy the best meal in town for around $1.25. That price even included dessert and drink. If you ordered a steak more than likely they would have to send out for it at the nearest meat market. Wages were very low. For example: the cashier at the bank was making $25.00 a week. The only bank in town was owned by Claude Fuller, (The Baron of the Ozarks). The dry cleaners paid their help around 17¢ an hour.

When we declared that we were going to build the Statue and the rest of the projects, most of the town folk said,"Yes, we have had many dreamers come to this town only to have their dreams vanish. We will wait and see!"

Our dreams have come true. Eureka Springs is now one of the wealthiest towns in the country for it's size. While the Play is open the town is alive and when we close, for the most part, so does the town. We certainly know that, GOD DID IT ALL!

Our first house in Eureka Springs

Our children, Kay, Brittarose,
Darlene and Chuck

Mrs. Smith, Baroness Maria von Trapp
and myself

Chapter Twelve

The Children

A FENCED BRAZEN WALL

Sometimes we stand at the threshold
    of challenge the enemy sends,
The forces of darkness surround us
    and it seems as our life they would end.

But Christ Jesus came that we might have
    life-life more abundantly.
So we'll turn from the challenge to Jesus,
    In Him is the victory.

He sends forth His word to comfort,
    Strenghten His child's faint heart.
I know when He says it, He'll do it.
    To harken and follow, this is my part.

He says, "I'll make unto this people,
    a fenced brazen wall",
The enemy may surround you,
    But you must stand bold and tall.

The enemy will fight you.
  But they shall not prevail.
My promise is to save you,
  and I will never fail.

Let God arise and let His enemies be scattered,
  As smoke is driven away.
Our God arose, the enemy's defeated.
  Praise God—the victory is ours today.

Kay Peterson
October 1981

After the Christ of the Ozarks statue had been completed, I knew that I had to talk with the Smiths about all of the long hours and days that I had been away from the family. In discussing with Mr. Smith the subject of the Foundation and all of the activities of the Smiths, I had come to the conclusion that physically I was no longer able to handle driving the long hours that it entailed when we were traveling. Often I would drive sixteen to eighteen hours a day and be away from home for weeks at a time.

"Mr. Smith, I feel that I can no longer keep the pace I have been keeping. Perhaps we should try to work out some other arrangements concerning my employment," I said.

That seemed to fit right into his program and he immediately responded, "Well, Charles, I was going to ask you and your wife to come here to Eureka Springs and take over the work of the Elna M. Smith Foundation. I know that neither of you has any idea what it is going to grow into at this moment. I know that I have discussed with you many things, but even I do not fully understand what the Lord has in His mind. I believe that if you are here on the grounds, however, these things will take shape much more quickly."

I began to realize then, that this is what God had spoken to me many years before when He said, "Charles,

I have a new work for you to do. Something that you have never done before."

I had many qualms about going back to California and telling Gunda that we should move to the hills of Eureka Springs, Arkansas. I knew that it was the will of God and so there was nothing else for me to do but simply blurt it out. So I returned to California and went into the house and said, "Gunda, it is the will of God that we move to Eureka Springs!"

She looked at me stunned and cried, "Oh honey, we can't! We can't! We have just gotten our home paid for and we are now going to be able at last to buy new furniture and fix it up like we have always dreamed of doing. Charles, it is such a lovely place and I enjoy it so much. We have worked hard for fifteen years to pay for it. And if we move to Eureka Springs, we will be leaving all of the children here on the West Coast. Darlene's wedding is only a few months away. Honey, are you certain this is the will of God?"

I thought for a few seconds and then I said, "Yes, honey, I know this is the will of God."

After Darlene's wedding we asked Chuck and his wife LaVonne to move into the house and watch over it for us. They hesitated, but finally agreed. It wasn't long, however, until they bought a home of their own and so we decided to sell our home and "burn all the bridges."

By this time all of the children were grown and married. We give thanks daily that they are all living for the Lord and serving Him. All of them for years had been working with us for the Smiths in the print shop or in the office.

I have really got to give Gunda the credit for guiding them through life. I was gone so much of the time that most of the responsibility was hers. They attended church and were very active in everything that went on as far as the youth were concerned. Each of them graduated from Bible school and one by one God selected for them their mate and they were married.

I was unaware how much my children suffered during

their school years for their father's taking a stand with Mr. Smith. Gunda did an excellent job in teaching them how to handle the situation. She often said to them, "Now look, children, what we are supposed to do is always remember to lift up Jesus Christ. What Mr. Smith and your father are doing is good and they have their convictions and their ministry and that is good. But always remember you are a Christian and you should do everything you can to lift up the Lord."

She tried to keep them on a level keel, she wouldn't let them get on one side or another. They had their lives to live on their own. She didn't make them come over to my way of thinking; she wanted them to make their own decisions. She taught them to suffer for Jesus not for any man. You don't suffer for a man, you suffer for the Lord. Kay and Brittarose often would come home and say, "Mother, all the other minister's kids are dancing and doing all these other things. Why can't we?" "Children," Gunda said, "Could you do that if the Lord was there? Would that be what God would want you to do? Don't do anything unless you feel you could take the Lord with you and you feel pleased with what you're doing." Many, many times it was hard for them because we lived a walk that we felt had to please the Lord all the time. There were times when it was very difficult, I am sure, to convince the children that we were right. However, we knew the Word of God to be true and we believed that if we trained our children (not anyone else), they would all live for and serve God.

This perhaps isn't in chronological order but each of them has written something about their childhood and coming here to Eureka Springs. Brittarose and her husband are no longer with the Foundation and now live in California.

KAY

"I was about three years old when I met Mr. and Mrs. Smith. He was such a huge man as I peeked at him over the back of the couch. That peek was the beginning of many times that I would see them in our home. Mother had taught us to respect people and we realized that Mr. and Mrs. Smith were Dad's employers. There were many times that we wanted to do certain things but Dad would have to excuse himself because he had obligations with the Smiths. Perhaps that was a little hard on us but we always seemed to get through it. It never was a major catastrophe. Even when Dad was gone on long trips, we would be so involved in our church activities that we would keep a pretty even schedule.

"Mom had to be very careful with the budget because the funds were very limited. I always went to the super market with Mom and I would try to add up everything as we put it in the cart. Mom made it a fun time and I enjoyed every minute of shopping.

"When Dad was home in the evenings, we would play Scrabble or other word games on that order. That was always a special time for me.

"Our friends considered our home very strict because we weren't allowed just to run loose. We all helped with the house work and each of us had responsibilities.

"Mom and Dad were strict with us but it certainly didn't hurt us. There were so many things we were involved in we had little time ever to feel sorry for ourselves. We didn't go to movies or dance, etc.

"My social life revolved around the church and Christian young people. So basically I had very little peer pressure to do wrong.

"The thing that I missed the most because of Dad's schedule, once I got into high school, was not being involved in the ball games. It didn't seem like a law, that was just the way it was. We really honored and respected our parents. The times that I would be home sick I would hear Mom praying and interceding for me. That made a big impression on me as a child. I grew up knowing that my Mom and Dad prayed for me. We had devotional times together but it wasn't like a church service in our home. We prayed and shared together. If we had a problem, we knew someone cared. I know that one of the most significant things that Mom and Dad taught us that God was real. He wasn't just a force but Someone who cared about us. It didn't matter what it was, we could take it to Him. Dad was always a very gentle person. One time I fell and cut my chin, I jumped and ran into the house. I was hysterical; Dad took me to the couch and carefully doctored by chin and prayed for me.

"Much of what I am today in Christ is because of the understanding that I gained as a child watching Mom and Dad. It is tremendous to know that I can go to God for anything. He touched my sister and she was well again. It is tremendous that I know God. Now as a mother, I know that when my child is sick and has a fever of 103°, I can go to the Lord about my child.

"Everything that Dad touched, God blessed. Like our home in Glendale, it was a gorgeous house, everybody thought that I lived in a mansion. I remember my friends coming in and saying, 'You live in a castle don't you.' That was God!

"Marvin, my husband, and I came to Eureka Springs on vacation in June of 1977. While we were here, it seemed like there was a tremendous burden so heavy you felt like you could reach out and touch it. On our way back to California we felt like God was saying that we should move to Eureka Springs. We pressed that down and said that it was fleshly desire saying that we wanted to be close to our parents. We started to analyze all the wonderful things that we had — the church, a beautiful congregation that loved us very much, etc. However, the more that we ministered, the more we knew that God was calling us to Eureka Springs.

"Near the Fourth of July we went to visit my sister. While we were there, we had a tremendous time. As we were driving home, God spoke to me saying, 'I've told you to go to Eureka Springs.' I turned to Marvin and said, 'Is God speaking to you like He is to me? Is God really saying to you that we should go to Eureka Springs?' Marvin looked at me somewhat surprised and said, 'That's what God is saying to me, too.'

"The date that kept coming to us was August the 20th. 'That is ridiculous,' I thought, 'why August the 20th?' But we went home and a couple of days later I called Mom and told her that we were moving to Eureka Springs. She said, 'Oh that's super.' She was really excited. An hour later she called me back and said that Dad told us not to come because there was no work for us. My reply was, 'Mom, we aren't coming because you asked us, but because God told us to. We are to be an inspiration and an encouragement to the believers. I don't know what God wants us to do. He may want us to start a church. He may even open a door for us to work at the Foundation. That is immaterial, we are moving because God told us to.' Marvin said, 'If indeed God has called us, we are to step out by faith and go.' So he called the elders and shared with them our moving. They said, 'This can't be, the church is growing, people are being saved, filled with the Holy Spirit and most of all we love you. No pastor leaves when things are going good.

Marvin called our district supervisor and said to him, 'Kay and I will be resigning effective August 12th. Will you come for our last Sunday?' There was a long, long silence. Then he said, 'Are you sure, brother, that is what God wants you to do?' And Marvin said, 'Dr. Jones, I have never been so sure of anything in all of my life.' He did all he could to talk us out of going. Even after our furniture had sold, and everything else was loaded in the trailer, a deacon said, 'If you kids will not go, I will buy all new furniture for your house.' A teenage girl came and said, 'Pastor we can't accept your going.' I said to her, 'How can you and the church be blessed if we stay and miss God?'

"A few days before we moved to Arkansas, the Lord spoke to Marvin to call Dad and give him, as a promise, a Bible verse. This was rather unusual for us, but we knew we had to obey the Lord.

"We called Dad and said, 'Dad, God has given you this promise found in Jeremiah 15:20, '*And I will make thee unto his people a fenced brazen wall: and they shall fight against thee, but they shall not prevail against thee: for I am with thee to save thee and to deliver thee, saith the Lord'.'*

"Dad said, 'I receive that.'

"We chatted awhile and then hung up.

"God had spoken to us and we heard Him. We arrived in Eureka Springs the day my father was served with a devastating lawsuit.

"About three weeks passed when Dad and Mrs. Smith called Marvin to the office and asked him if we would have lunch with them. They asked him if he would help with the Foundation and he said he would. Later on in that year they asked Marvin if he would serve with the Board of Directors. That was the beginning of our involvement. We worked during the day and counseled with some of the employees that were filled with confusion. How I praise God that he brought us there to be a help in a time of need. God has been good to us. The lawsuit was resolved.

"Marvin and I are very much involved in the Foundation and all of its projects. How I personally thank God for parents who put God first and showed, by example, how I could do the same."

DARLENE

"Mom and Dad, as I look back, you really had us in the Word of God. So, when the problems came, we knew to turn them over to the Lord. I guess that is the reason all four of us kids chose to attend the same Bible College that you, Mom, and Grandmother Britta went to.

"When I became ill as a child of seven with polio, you turned it all over to the Lord and He healed me. What a great lesson that was for later in life when the doctors told me that I had a terminal brain tumor. Darla and Vonda were only five and six years old. But, again, because of your training, I knew right away to take the whole problem to the Lord. Saturday, in the middle of the night while I was praying, before surgery, the Lord spoke to my heart and told me that He was in control and He flooded my spirit with peace. And, God did take care of me — He did heal me! That was back in 1976.

"Dad, I never resented all of your traveling. I knew you were serving the Lord and you always stayed in touch by phone.

"As young people, we were always busy doing the things of the Lord. Chuck was the camp director and worked with the young people at the church, so at an early age we were all involved with summer camps and church. That was also great training for the future.

"One winter I flew to Eureka Springs to serve as Mr. Smith's secretary for a few months. This was during the time he was purchasing the property for the Christ of the Ozarks and the Great Passion Play. I was named as the Recording Secretary for the Foundation at that time.

"Mom and Dad, I can remember, as a small child discussing the fact that communism was trying to destroy America and that if communism ever took over, our Bibles would be taken away. As a result we knew the importance of reading our Bibles and memorizing verses.

"God gave me a wonderful husband by the name of Kenneth Smith, and as I mentioned earlier, two beautiful children, Darla and Vonda. We lived in California and Ken was the head of the Math Department at Alhambra High School. We had a lovely home and were very content. However, when we were told how much work there was in Eureka Springs, producing the Passion Play, we came to help.

"Mom and Dad, you mean everything to me. Both of you have taught me to put Jesus first in my life. We love you!"

CHUCK

"From the time we moved to California in 1943, Dad was gone much of the time. And so through experimentation, I learned to build my own scooter, and to fix this and fix that. When I was only eight, I started to work in Grandma's print shop. Dad and Mom were working there, too. Dad was finishing his degree at L.I.F.E. Bible College. Working in the print shop helped expose me to a lot of mechanical things, and the salary helped to buy my clothes.

"Because of the continuing involvement with Mr. Smith from the mid-forties, our family developed a sense of isolation. Instead of running with my buddies after school, I had to come straight home. As a result, I went into a shell of almost constant reading. I would read ten to twelve books a week. I read everything. The library was a block away, and was one place that I could go. As a result of all of my reading, I was exposed to what was going on in the world. It made me value things differently, made me more flexible, and able to accept other people's ideas and still have my own.

"I was excited when we moved to the high desert community of Independence, California, during the summer of 1951 because I now had the desert and the high Sierras to explore. For the first few months, Dad was only home on the weekends so we learned to survive in every phase of our lives without him. Mom was very strong and spent much of her time helping formulate our moral and spiritual values. I personally feel that without her stability, prayers and guidance, I would have gotten into trouble. But Mom was always there; as solid as the Rock of Gibraltar.

"During our second year in the desert, Dad became a fulltime employee of Mr. Smith and traveled extensively. Then in May, 1952, we moved to Glendale, California to be near the Smiths and operate their print shop. The print shop was in part of our home and I worked there during high school and while completing my degree at L.I.F.E. Bible College. From 1960 until 1969, I was responsible for all the printing needs of Mr. Smith including his magazine and book publishing. I was content in knowing God was using our efforts through our work and our extra activities such as pastoring and church youth work.

"In 1968, God began dealing with me to return to college and get a degree in business and accounting which I completed in 1970. In 1975, God opened the doors for us to move to the high desert community of Bishop, California which was only 45 miles north of Independence which had produced so many pleasant memories.

"God used our years in Bishop to affect a number of lives for Him and to give me additional business, political, spiritual and emotional experiences to better prepare me for later responsibilities. We bought an accounting practice when we moved to Bishop and also started a computer service bureau and an interdenominational church in a nearby ranch and mining community.

"In 1981, God directed me to sell both businesses and I thought he wanted me to be the fulltime pastor at the church we had started and built. God had different plans, and while recovering from a kidney stone operation, He assured me I was to come to Arkansas for a time and assist dad at the foundation.

The influence of my parents, relatives and friends helped to establish my standards and values. Involvement in church and its activities helped to keep me from undesirable mischief.

"My main purpose in life is like that of my parents; to serve the Lord to the fullest of my abilities wherever I am."

BRITTAROSE

I am grateful for the privilege of being born and reared in a Christ centered home.

Our childhood was basically happy. Of course, we experienced our share of good times and bad, joys and sorrows, ups and downs. We were taught that regardless of the circumstance, God was in control. That He is our friend Who never leaves us nor forsakes us. He gives life purpose and meaning, and He calls us all into service to carry the good news into all the world.

It is our responsibility to seek God and find out His will for us and then to carry out our findings. I believe He leads us when we submit to that leading. This is a great gift for which I am most grateful to God and my parents.

On day of two millionth visitor
Marvin Peterson, Gunda, myself and
Mr. and Mrs. Eagle Thomas

"Mr. Mayor" in a parade

Chapter Thirteen

The Great Passion Play

When we arrived in Eureka Springs, we found ourselves a little home and again in my busyness, Gunda took the task of painting, plastering, wallpapering and remodeling, especially the downstairs rooms. I was so very busy, oftentimes I'm sure, she thought she was a widow and the children thought they had lost their father. It was at this time in 1964 the Foundation that was to be called the Elna M. Smith Foundation was born. By the time we received our tax exempt status from the Internal Revenue Service, the statue had been completed. Mr. Smith through the years had collected fine antiques and paintings and little did he realize that God would prosper the purchase of these, that his vision might be fulfilled on Mt. Oberammergau and Magnetic Mountain.

The Smiths often referred to me as their son even though they had adopted a son and he was loved very much by them and he loved them. However, he was not at all interested in what they were doing, so he went his own way. Therefore I had a great deal of influence with them and they had the utmost confidence in me.

Mr. Smith was very concerned that the Foundation be set up in such a way that nobody could invade it and take away the contents, the dream and the vision. All their worldly possessions were therefore transferred to the Foundation so there never could be any contest of their desires. Whatever the Foundation is today is because they put seed faith in it, inspired it and established it. Many of their friends also financially helped them.

As Mr. Smith began to elaborate on all the things he had in mind. my faith started welling up within me and was kindled quickly. I realized that he was proposing a project that would be so elaborate and extensive that it would be known world wide. I was thrilled, as I was to be an intricate part of the entire project.

I was co-founder of the project as Mrs. Smith's name and mine were on all the papers of the Foundation. Mr. Smith's name did not appear there. Mrs. Smith's sister, Nan Nearhoff, was also a part of the Foundation and our daughter, Darlene, was listed as recording secretary. So my daughter also was there at the very beginning.

Mr. Smith shared with me in detail what he anticipated. I was privileged to receive information that he had only shared with his wife. He was always very closed-mouth on what he expected the Foundation actually to accomplish. Mr. Smith was determined that God would fulfill the Bible promises, "*When the enemy came in like a flood, that He would lift up a standard against him.*" He wanted to establish for the Lord a witness in the midst of the land. I really had never put the two together until the day that he marked the "X" on the ground where we were going to build the monument to Christ. I realized then that a witness for the Lord was really going to be established in the midst of the land. As far as that is concerned, in the midst of the world to bear witness of the Lord Jesus Christ. It was then that I realized to the fullest THAT GOD HAD

INDEED CALLED ME TO A NEW WORK. After the statue was completed, Mr. Smith began talking about The Great Passion Play. His vision almost overwhelmed me. We went back to the land and we began to explore it. We walked up one hill and down the other looking for the site of the huge amphitheater. It almost seemed hopeless. All of the large trees had long before been used for timber so this was second growth and the mountains were almost impassible. Yet as we stood on one point of Mt. Oberammergau, we looked down and there you could see the natural amphitheater.

All that needed to be done was the simple task of clearing the land, setting the staging area and then building the city of Jerusalem on one side of the mountain and a seating arrangement on the other. That seemed all quite simple, at least to Mr. Smith.

We planned to open early in July of 1968. The bulldozers worked feverishly and it did seem quite simple at times. Everything seemed to have been pre-arranged by God Himself. The seating area was cut out layer upon layer, tier upon tier, so the concrete could be poured establishing the steps for the seating arrangement. We were ready to pour the concrete, but it seemed like Satan certainly didn't want the play to open. In the month of July which normally is a very dry time of year in the Ozarks, we had delay upon delay because of thirty-six inches of rain. One day there was a six inch rain and in hours the water washed most of our terraced dirt away. The concrete of course could not be poured and the tiers had to again be developed, which was very costly. However, we did open and had a total attendance of about 28,000 the first year.

The Great Passion Play is the original Ozarks Passion Play. It is performed in a 4,400 seat amphitheater. The cast of the Great Passion Play includes nearly two hundred people and many live animals, common to the Holy Land during Christ's life on earth. The set, the staging, the lighting and sound system combine to present what is often called the nation's number one outdoor drama.

The Great Passion Play brings to life the glory and the triumph of the life, crucifixion, resurrection and ascension of Jesus Christ. Many individuals and groups return year after year to experience the inspiration of this powerful performance.

I will never forget as we sat there for the first time as the procession began and the Word was spoken, *"If I be lifted up, I will draw all men unto Me."* We prayed, "Oh, God! Let it be so that many will find Jesus as their Saviour as they view this great production of the last days of Jesus on the face of the earth."

The second year 58,000 attended and it has grown every year since. The Great Passion Play is done in a six month season. It begins on the last Friday in April and closes the last Saturday of October.

Many, many stories and testimonies have been shared because of the Great Passion Play. You see, the entire production is the spoken Word directly from the Bible. No one can sit and view the play through its entirety and say they have never heard the way to Jesus; they are without excuse. Many have found Christ as Saviour. There have been those freed from drugs while they listened, marriages put together, drunks sobered and lives transformed. In the year 1985 we celebrated the visit of our three millionth guest. We are constantly endeavoring to improve the lighting, the costumes and the staging that it will bring glory to Jesus.

Mr. and Mrs. Smith devoted their time entirely to the Lord's work. Lecturing, writing, and telling the facts as they were. Neither one smoked, drank, or indulged in worldly activities that the average person does. Their recreation was visiting antique stores, perhaps to make a purchase or just to get the shop keeper to tell them about a particular antique. They learned early in their lives the value of the beautiful and antique pieces. Thus their collection through the years was a combination of what one would call sleepers. They would go into an antique shop, and Mr. Smith seemed to have a super sense of looking around and almost at a glance picking out that unique and unusual item. He would ask, "What is this?" When they would say, "I don't know," and he did, he was able at times to obtain quality items at ridiculously low prices.

It was this antique collection that produced much of what is on the mountain top today. As the amphitheater was being built and as more money was needed, they sold their home in Tulsa as well as all the contents and put the total amount into the construction of the amphitheater. He was a man who was very generous and a man who knew where he was going and he had the persuasive ability to persuade others to join him in accomplishing whatever he set out to do.

The purpose of the Great Passion Play is to tell the passion of our Lord Jesus Christ and to re-enact it in such a way that it gives the audience the feeling that they are beholding the actual event. There have been those in the audience who have stood to their feet during the flogging of Jesus and have cried out, "Stop it, stop it!" They so felt that they were right there with the mob as our Lord was being scourged. I can remember several years ago when Baroness Maria von Trapp came with her publisher to view The Great Passion Play. After the play was finished, she asked if she could meet the cast. We ushered her to the main street of Jerusalem and she greeted the apostles even kissing them one by one until she came to Judas. She then said with a chuckle in her voice, "I'm sorry, Judas, I just can't kiss you after what you've done to my Jesus." She requested to meet the girl who had played Mary. After the introduction the girl turned to Baroness von Trapp and said, "Baroness, did you enjoy the play?" We were amazed and awestruck as this woman of great renown turned to the girl and said, "Enjoy! My dear, I was there!" It was then that we knew that God had permitted us to do what we longed to do. Take people back to those very days that Christ walked on earth.

The dedication and devotion of Mr. and Mrs. Smith were pure and constant. They sat at the entrance to the

Passion Play night after night every year until Mr. Smith's death and Mrs. Smith continued to do the same. Although they are missed tremendously, they are also remembered. How two people could give everything so completely is beyond the comprehension of many, but then they believed that they were to "Take up His cross and follow Him." They could see no turning back, but a steady going forward.

Stage of The Great Passion Play

The Apostles listen to Christ
The Great Passion Play

Christ speaks on steps of Temple
The Great Passion Play

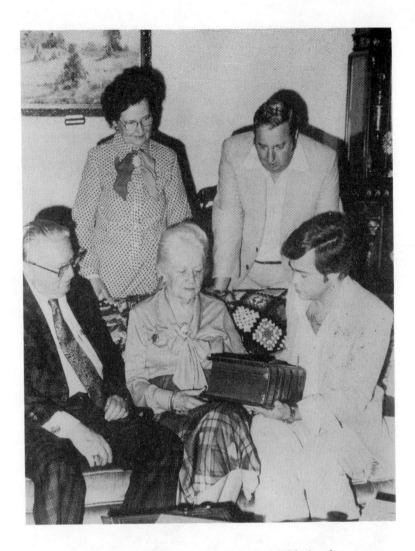

Jim Bakker presents Mrs. Smith a Bible for the
Museum as Gunda, Cliff Dudley and I look on

Board Members of Elna M. Smith Foundation
(Marvin Peterson absent)

Twentieth Anniversary of Elna M.
Smith Foundation

Chapter Fourteen

Moving The Mountains

LOOKING UNTO JESUS

A challenge stands before me,
*   A mountain stretching high—*
It seems so overwhelming,
*   The question, How will I pass by?*

If I worry, scheme or figure,
*   The mountain—only seems to grow.*
So I'll fix my eyes on Jesus
*   And trust Him the path to show.*

He says 'If I have the faith
*   Of a grain of mustard seed,*
I can say unto this mountain
*   Be cast into the sea'.*

As I stand in faith and courage,
*   This mountain can not stay.*
Jesus bids me steadily forward,
*   He knows and leads the way.*

Mountains are not impassible,
If you know Christ the Lord of all,
He's reaching out to help you.
If you need Him, only call.

In love, strength and wisdom
He'll stay right by your side,
He'll lift you when you've fallen,
He'll be your constant guide.

Look up, keep your eyes on Jesus,
The mountain is not so tall
Follow when He leads you,
By grace—He conquers all.

Kay Peterson
September 1981

I Chronicles 28:20
Be strong and courageous and get to work.
Don't be frightened by the size of the task, for
the Lord my God is with you; He will not for-
sake you. He will see to it that everything is
finished correctly.

Following the completion of the giant statue. THE CHRIST OF THE OZARKS, and the establishment of The Great Passion Play, it was decided by the Smiths to donate their collection of portrayals of Christ to humanity through the Elna M. Smith Foundation. Thus as the visiting public come to see The Great Passion Play, they can take advantage of the fruits of a lifetime of dedication in viewing this collection.

THE CHRIST ONLY ART GALLERY

There are over 1,000 portrayals of our Lord. In-cluded are objects so rare and so sensational that one of the objects would be worth the visit. The viewer should observe that the collection is representative of every field of art, including the masterpieces, the provincial manifestation of Christian faith, rare and unusual prints, oil painting on copper, brass, tin, porcelain, wood, and glass.

Our most recent additions to the Gallery are two paintings by Charles Vickery, *"Jesus Walking on the Sea"* and *"Jesus"*. Also, Rev. and Mrs. Samuel Stearman have placed the painting *"The Baptism of Jesus"* by Alderman Joseph Brook of Huddersfield, England in 1874 in our Gallery. The Southern Baptist convention have used this picture on their Baptismal Certificate for many years.

You can come and take a guided tour and the curators will enlighten you as to some of the objects and then you can tour on your own after you have had the opportunity to hear the guides and if you have other questions to ask, they will be very happy to answer them. Often people have asked, "Why isn't this art in New York?" We're thankful that the Lord saw fit to put it in Eureka Springs, Arkansas, which is almost the population center of the United States. The purpose of the Gallery is to bring the message of Christ as seen through the eye of the Artist.

We are believing God today to supply us with funds to buy twenty-two 17th century works of art that are mostly of Christ. This would give us the most complete religious collection of art this side of New York City.

THE BIBLE MUSEUM AND
SMITH MEMORIAL CHAPEL

The Smith Memorial Chapel was built so our guests could come to pray and meditate. There are daily sacred concerts given there during the summer season.

The great altar sculpture in the chapel is believed to be a Raphael.

Because our Bible Collection is so rare and irreplaceable, it was decided that the foundation and lower level of the chapel be built in a vault like manner. It is there we now have the Bible Museum.

The Smith Memorial Chapel is located on Mt. Oberammergau. The Bible Museum contains the largest number of old Bibles (7,000 volumes) and ancient sacred writings (3,000 primitive manuscripts and artifacts) ever to be assembled into a private single collection. These rare documents represent over 625 languages.

Some items are so priceless, irreplaceable and valuable that they must be stored in vaults for security purposes.

An official appraiser of such documents for the Congressional Library, who is a professional student of historic books and sacred writings, Dr. Fred McGraw, considers this to be one of the two greatest collections of sacred scriptures to be found anywhere on earth.

Many Bibles in the collection have been used by the Hallmark Greeting Card Co. as photographic models.

More than 6,000 clergymen and religious leaders of all denominations have been invited to view the exhibit as it contains certain historic documents that are of unusual interest to scholars.

Some of the highlights of the collection are: Volumes written by hand before the invention of the printing press.

Most important facsimile of the first Bible printed — the Gutenberg. An original is valued at approximately two million dollars.

Most important facsimile of the first edition of the King James Version.

Most important translation into the Cherokee Indian language. Twenty-five hundred segments valued in the commercial world at one hundred thousand dollars.

A large type set requiring seven volumes.

A 16th century Hymnal.

Danish Pastoral letter dated 1442.

A Babylonian cuneiform cone.

Egyptian primitive documents illuminated.

Engraving of the Lord's Prayer on a metal segment

one-sixth of an inch square.

The only Gideon Bible signed by all the founding officers of the Gideon Society.

Every important translation of the Bible — Catholic, Protestant and Greek — is represented in the collection.

The famous Breeches Bible printed in 1589 in Geneva.

A Polyglot Bible containing the full Bible in twelve languages, begun in 1657 in Cambridge, England.

The Walton Polyglot Bible printed in England by Roycraft at the order of Oliver Cromwell in 1627.

First run of Quaker Bible — 1764.

First Catholic Bible printed in England in 1617.

The first Vellum manuscript from France, eleven centuries old.

1861 — Civil War New Testament and Psalms.

Isaiah Thomas Bible — 1791 — first edition of the first folio edition printed in the United States. Isaiah Thomas was a friend of Benjamin Franklin.

Thomas Jefferson Bible — reprint 1923.

The Bible, God's Holy Word, has been recorded throughout the centuries in several languages and on a variety of materials. These include, clay, stone, lead, bronze, gold, ivory, bone, wood, wax, linen, papyrus, leather, vellum, parchment and paper. Many of these materials are found in this sensational collection.

PARABLES OF THE BIBLE
FROM THE POTTER'S HOUSE

There are several pre-play performances, one of which is given by "the Potter." He demonstrates by making a pot upon the potter's wheel, as he tells how that clay must be refined, how it must be shaped and then be trimmed. Then after it is made it has to pass through the fire. It is no good until it is fired. Even as believers in Christ we must pass through the fire to be refined. It really is quite a story.

WOOD CARVING GALLERY

We also have an Inspirational Wood Carving Gallery

that contains many carvings, all scenes from the life of Christ, by the late Cecil Mount.

THE NEW HOLY LAND

One of the newest projects of the Foundation is "The New Holy Land." Why The New Holy Land? With wars, the unrest and upheavals in the world, the Holy Land is rapidly becoming off bounds for Christians and tourists. There are millions of people in the United States that cannot afford to travel overseas. Many also do not have the time to enjoy the inspiration of the Holy Land. As we re-construct it on the property of the Foundation, it comes into the reach of everyone. Yes, there will have to be a charge made to pay for the guides, the maintenance and for security, but it will be kept at a minimal amount. It is not intended for monetary profit, but as a teaching tool for every Sunday School teacher, every minister and every layman. It is believed that as people come and hear the Sermon on the Mount, the message on the Mount of Olives, or the Prayer in the Garden of Gethsemane that hearts will be touched. Or perhaps those standing before the three crosses on Golgatha will be reminded of where the Son of God was suspended between Heaven and Earth as He was rejected by man, yet held to the cross by your sin and mine. There will be multitudes of souls spoken to there by the Spirit of God.

The New Holy Land will take many years and many, many donations to accomplish its construction as it was when Christ was upon the earth. Of course the Sea of Galilee and the Jordon River are in miniature, but most of the buildings will be life size. Perhaps some of the huge structures will be reduced in scale but not enough to take away from the impressiveness of them.

The New Holy Land development is coming along very nicely. It's slow, but we are paying for it as we build. We'd love to have some people take some of these projects and sponsor them.

At the present time we have completed the Nativity and placed three Italian marble figures of Christ in the New Holy Land. We have the Mount of Olives, the Sermon on the Mount, the Garden of Gethesemane, the Tomb, Golgotha, the Sea of Galilee, and the Jordon River. In the Jordon River we are preparing a baptismal area where any church can come and have their baptismal services.

As the temple is built, there will be an auditorium in it so we can portray all of the incidents that took place around the temple when Christ was here on earth. It will be scaled down slightly. I believe the original doorway was sixty-five feet high; we will scale it down so the doorway will be fifty feet high. We will be building Solomon's temple in preference to building Herod's temple. Solomon's temple has much more spiritual significance. We will add the courtyard at a later date as the funds are received.

There will also be the Upper Room building which will also contain an auditorium. The main feature of the Upper Room will be the second floor where we will have a portrayal of the Last Supper. The third floor will be the Upper Room where the Holy Spirit was given on the day of Pentecost.

Mr. Smith laid out thirty sites that he felt we ought to have in The New Holy Land. He said, "Charles, this will take you a few years to accomplish and it will take all of the money the Lord sends in or the Foundation makes. No one will have to wonder what to do with the money. The New Holy Land will dictate the spending of the Foundation's money for years to come."

The plaque in front of the Eastern Gate, the entrance to The New Holy Land, contains the names of those who have donated one thousand dollars or more to the project. We are not selling recognition, but we do want to recognize those who do participate.

The terrain is very similar to that of the Holy Land. There are even dogwood and red bud trees like they have in the Holy Land. There are cattails like those along the Nile River where Moses was hid in the bulrushes. Shortly the Dead Sea will be developed, increasing our water mass greatly. We have two buses and two vans at the present time that transport people down the mountain to The New Holy Land. There will be no cars allowed. So far, this year we have had over 19,000 visit The New Holy Land. Without exception they've all returned very excited. Many have expressed the desire to linger and meditate there. That of course is our desire also.

The Elna M. Smith Foundation, a charitable religious educational organization, fulfilled the Smiths' desires until his death April 15, 1976 and Elna's on May 21, 1981. They are interred in a crypt just below the left arm of the Christ of the Ozarks. A fitting resting place for two people who have given so much to the world in honor of the Lord Jesus Christ whom they loved so very much.

The following statement was prepared for the occasion of Mr. and Mrs. Smith's fiftieth Wedding Anniversary on June 12, 1972 and reflects their attitude towards life:

"No one should boast of the blissful gift of marital compatibility. It is God's gift, but there are some fundamental ways to facilitate and keep alive this beautiful attribute of life.

"I cannot remember a day my husband failed to express his love for me in word or deed or both.

"Mutual respect is the solvent that helps us to bear with each other's mistakes.

"I have always been intrigued by what my husband had to say in public and elsewhere. He tells me that I have been his most interested listener. I have never become calloused to his activities.

"Although we have always had a good cook, I like to demonstrate my ability to cook in preparing something especially tasteful.

"We have both recognized the unique place of man and the special calling of a woman. Every happy marriage should consist of two masters and two slaves. I cannot imagine denying a request from my husband and I cannot imagine his declining to fulfill my desires.

"On the day of our wedding, fifty years ago, my husband's sweet and aging grandmother came to the altar of the church after the wedding and said to my husband of about five minutes, 'Always remember, Gerald, the woman doesn't live who has been loved too much.'

"Of course our Christian faith has given the comfort, the vision, and the strength to carry on. Prayer is the miracle which permits us to visit with our Creator. This gift makes it possible for human beings to operate with instructions from headquarters every day.

"Common ideals — Christian faith and our love of beauty as art collectors, have combined to make our lives very fulfilling.

"At seventy-five years of age we are great believers in vital activity as against retirement.

"It has been one beautiful honeymoon — so much so that we both pray that when the summons comes, we can go together."

Garden Tomb in The New Holy Land

"Peter", myself and Gunda
First actor in The New Holy
Land, Fred McWhorter

The Christ Only Art Gallery

Potter at work

Smith Memorial Chapel

The Church in the Wildwood that
contained our first Bible Museum

The Bible Museum

The Great Eastern Gate and
one of the play's camels

The Christ of the Ozarks

Governor Orville Faubaus and myself

Our family, 1985

Chapter Fifteen

God Cares

All of our children Chuck, Brittarose, Darlene and Kay have been wonderfully blessed and used of the Lord. My wife and I rejoice every day that God has called them one by one into the tremendous ministry of the Elna M. Smith Foundation. All of them have very important and vital roles in the over-all project. I do not fail to give thanks to God every day for this miracle.

I know that the key to our childrens' success as far as God is concerned was the faithfulness of my wife. From the very first moment we were married we put everything on the altar. We committed everything to God, most of all our children. When God told Abraham to offer up his only son Isaac, Abraham put the very best that he had on the altar. If God had not intervened, Abraham would have made the supreme sacrifice. That has been the principal of our whole lives. Put everything and everyone upon the altar of God. That makes Christ supreme in one's life. We have watched all our children pass through all the regular childhood diseases and the Lord has cared for each and every one of them. There are, however, some extreme miracles that the Lord has performed for them, my wife and also for me.

Our oldest child Chuck, was driving home from Los Angeles where he worked for the Farmers Insurance Company on Wilshire Boulevard. He was coming off of the freeway preparing to turn on to a major highway, heading toward his home, when another large car which never saw him ran right over him. The wreck pinned him in the car where he was unable to move his legs. He had lacerations over most of his body and some of his main arteries had been severed. However, God had a doctor who had just finished surgery looking out the window of a nearby hospital. He saw the wreck, grabbed the nurses and said, "Let's go." They came running out of the hospital and were able to give Chuck the emergency care that he needed as he was pinned there in the car. Chuck had to be cut out of the car which took almost an hour. If the doctor hadn't been at that window, at that moment, without a doubt Chuck would have bled to death. Although he had over a hundred plus stitches in his face and neck, he doesn't show any scars today except one thin one. He has totally recovered. How we praise God that He took care of our son and brought him through that ordeal.

Nine years ago when our daughter Darlene was visiting us here in Eureka Springs she said, "Mom and dad, when I get home I'm going to have my eyes tested. There's something bothering me."

None of us thought much about it and when she returned to California, she went to the eye doctor to have her eyes checked. Much to her surprise he said, "Darlene, you've got to see your doctor immediately. I'll call and make the arrangements. Who is your family doctor?" At that he made the arrangements. He explained to the doctor what he had seen in her eyes. Her doctor had tests run and then contacted a neurologist. He told her she had a brain tumor and sent her right to the hospital. As soon as Darlene arrived at the hospital, they ran more tests and their fears were confirmed. She had a brain tumor. Surgery was scheduled for two days later. We received a call from her doctor here in Arkansas. He was very blunt and told us that if we wanted to see Darlene alive, we had better come and come immediately.

We took the next flight out preparing to be by her side. My wife had sent Darlene, some time earlier, two books that had blessed her. They were *Like A Mighty Wind* and *Gentle Breeze of Jesus*. These books instilled faith in her. She had written down many scriptures in her Bible that the Lord had impressed upon her and gave them to us and said, "I want you to read these scriptures while I'm in the operating room. Mom and dad, don't worry, everything is going to be all right."

Her doctor came to us and very seriously said, "Mr. and Mrs. Robertson, I want you to know that this is a very serious situation. The tumor is very large and if everything goes well, the most you can expect your daughter to live is six months. If we don't operate immediately she will most likely be blind in two days. Very shortly after that she will be paralyzed and it will go from bad to worse until she is gone. On the other hand, if I operate, there is only about a 15% chance that we can help her, and 85% that we can't. If we want to give her any extension of life at all, we must operate. Then we won't give her over a year or two to live at the most." We gave him our blessing and said, "Don't worry doctor, everything will be all right." He had also talked to Darlene very frankly and she wasn't upset. Her remark was, "Jesus healed me when I had polio, and He can heal me now."

As they were taking her into the operating room, the doctor stopped and again said to her, "Darlene, you don't seem to realize how serious this is and your parents certainly don't realize the seriousness of this." "Doctor," replied Darlene, "I'm in the hands of the Lord. Whatever He wants, that's the way it will be." Darlene's husband, Ken Smith, was there by the gurney and said, "Let's pray now that the Lord will guide your hands, doctor." At that Ken reached out and touched the doctor and prayed. I don't know if the doctor had anyone do that before, but he was astounded. He paused, then said, "Darlene and Ken, I want you to know how serious this is." Darlene looked up and smiled and said, "Doctor, everythings's fine." At that, he gave a look of total dismay and they went to the operating room.

The surgery took four and a half hours. We waited and waited and after what seemed like an eternity the doctor finally came to us. "It took me quite frankly a while before I had the courage to come and talk to you. My dear friends, I wasn't able to do anything. We opened up the cranium, but the tumor was a blanket tumor. It has integrated itself into the entire cranium. It's hard and none of it could be removed. The optical nerve is impacted and the artery to the brain also is totally impacted. We could not touch any part of it. I am so sorry, it is just a matter of time until the blood will be shut off completely to the brain. We had to close her back up. I wanted to wait to see if she would even survive the surgery and what her reactions would be. I must admit that I am totally flabbergasted to report that she has feeling back and is able to move all the members of her body. She can see and she seems to be in excellent condition. We can't understand it because we didn't do one single thing for her. She is in intensive care and most likely will have to stay there for a minimum of six weeks and we should keep her here in the hospital for probably three months." He turned to Ken and told him how he would have to get someone to take care of the children, etc.

Darlene went into intensive care about midnight and about two a.m. she was awake and talking to an attendant, which in this particular case was a male. She said to him, "I'm hungry, I want something to eat." "Something to eat!" he exclaimed. "You can't have anything to eat." "Well, I'm hungry. Before I came in here, I put a couple of candy bars in my suitcase. Please give me one of those." "Are you kidding? I wouldn't dare!" he said. "Well, there are two bars. If you give me one, I'll give you the other," she said. If you're that hungry I will put a call in to the doctor," he said. So at two a.m. he called her doctor and the doctor said, "Give her anything she wants, nothing matters at this point. She won't live anyway."

She was securely strapped down so she couldn't move her head subconsciously. He broke the candy and laid it on her chest so she could get it into her mouth. She consumed every morsel of it and relaxingly went to sleep, with the attendant wondering if she would be alive by morning. When they came to her room in the morning, she told them that she wanted breakfast. They brought her a few liquids which she ate quickly. Then she said to the attendant, "I've got to have something more than that. I'm really hungry." Again, because they thought it wouldn't make any difference, they brought her solid foods. That didn't satisfy her so she had her third breakfast. When the doctor came to see her, it was quite obvious to all that he was perplexed, puzzled and just plain astounded. Instead of their keeping her in intensive care for six weeks, she was moved to a regular hospital room in two days. Instead of her being in the hospital for months, they sent her home in less than a week. She went home and started caring for her house and her children. God in His divine mercy, healed her. Darlene is still working for the Lord. Not in California, but in Eureka Springs.

Our oldest daughter, Brittarose, has four children and wasn't supposed to have any after her second. She has had three caesarean. The doctor said definitely on the fourth child that the child wouldn't live and he doubted that Brittarose would. He strongly recommended an abortion. She wouldn't hear to that and said, "God is in control." Not only was that child born, but is now seven years old.

Our youngest daughter Kay has one testimony after another how God has taken care of her and the family.

When she and her husband Marvin Peterson were pastoring in California, their little daughter came in contact with a disease that was in the balloons that were sent up from Japan during the Second World War. Every now and then one of these balloons will be discovered. It is decomposed but the germs are still very active. Here again, the doctors didn't know quite how to treat her because she had so many different symptoms. They would treat this and something else would pop up. She was getting lifeless and colorless. After prayer and much faith, God touched that little child. Today she is very active doing gymnastics and all sorts of sports.

In a very humble way we are a family of miracles of God. I believe that God doesn't love us any more than He loves anyone else. He isn't a respector of persons but He does want lives that are committed entirely to Him.

Gunda was stricken with a back problem. We took her to the doctor to have it diagnosed and he said it was a ruptured disk. Later, she had begun to swell. So we took her back to the doctor and asked him to check her back and do something for her. The doctor put her in the hospital and said they would do more testing. They started testing her for one thing and another. They ran a light into her stomach and into her liver. They also took a biopsy of the liver. They put her through all kinds of X rays and tests and finally said, "Nothing shows up. You will have to go to Fayetteville and have a cat scan." So we did. We went back to see what the outcome was. They said that they hadn't discovered anything yet. "But we are going to send her somewhere else for more tests."

I said, "Well what are you going to do about her back?" They said, "There's been a vertebra fractured since the ruptured disk. Her back is deteriorating. It is very bad; however, there is nothing we can do about it." I said, "Well, that's what we brought her here for to begin with was to do something about her back." There's nothing we can do for her back. She'll just have to have complete bed rest for that. We need to run more tests," they said. I responded, "No more tests. If bed rest is what she is going to have to have for her back, then that's what we'll do first." "Oh, but she has cancer!" they said. "No way, you haven't found anything in there. All you say is that her body is swelling, she is accumulating water in her system and you haven't done anything. We're finished as far as the hospital is concerned." I exclaimed.

I took her home. We then went over to Springdale to a chiropractor and he said to Gunda, "All of your organs have stopped functioning because of your back. There is probably nothing else wrong as of the moment, but unless we get those organs to function, you will have very serious problems." He told her to take calcium and Vitamin C and juices. So we took her home, did what he said and prayed. We had others pray for her also. For about six months there we had to drag her to the rest room and drag her back to bed as she couldn't walk alone. It took time, but again, God in His love delivered her.

The other day we went back to see her doctor, he asked, "You haven't had any more problems with your liver have you?" Gunda said, "No, I haven't had any other problems. My back is getting stronger." He said, "The doctors in Fayetteville said you were supposed to have cancer."

We don't know if she had cancer or not, but she doesn't now! Praise the Lord!

Obviously God still has work for her to do.

One day we were at Eureka Inn for lunch. While eating, I had a strange sensation in my feet. They felt like they were burning and everything turned off. I tried to draw their attention, but I couldn't. I reached in my pocket to get a little box so I could pound on the table and I couldn't get my hand back out of my pocket. My heart had stopped! Kay's baby had taken their attention at the moment. When my wife looked at me, she could see my eyes were dilating and she could tell that I had no control at all, so she said, "Call the ambulance, quick!" A fireman who was sitting across the dining room saw what was happening. He came over and picked me up out of the chair. I was able to say to him, "I'm not choking." He said, "I know. I'll take care of you." He got my heart started, I don't know how, but he got me going again. I had revived to a degree so when the medics got there, they didn't know if I was choking or what. So we convinced them to take me to the hospital. They got me to the hospital and they put me on the monitor right away. While they were talking to me, I said, "Don't leave, don't leave. I can feel it coming again." As I said that my heart stopped again.

Gunda is now telling the story: "The doctor saw that and he said 'Look, his heart has stopped!' He called a code blue and they came real quick and started it again. The doctor said, 'We must take him to Springdale.' He called the hospital and said, 'Prepare for a pacemaker. The only thing we can do is put in a pacemaker.' On the way to Springdale about fifty miles away, his heart stopped three time. As he came into the hospital, the doctor cut his shirt open and said to the nurse, 'Take him to pre-op and get him prepared. No, just take him right to the operating room, we've got to put the pacemaker in immediately." So they took Charles right into the operating room. As they were working on him in surgery, his heart stopped three times again. The doctor had given him a local anesthetic for the operation. But he didn't know anything about it.

When I came to, the doctor asked, "Mr. Robertson, how do you feel?" I said, "I'm ready to go in." "Oh, it's all over. How do you feel?" he asked again. I said, "All right, but I feel a little strange." He said, "That's all right, your pacemaker is working. Your heart stopped three times while we were putting the pacemaker in so I know it's working." They released me Monday morning. By Monday noon I was back at the Eureka Inn for lunch. Three days after my Friday meal there. God still has more for me to do for Him and Gunda and I give Jesus Christ all the honor and glory for whatever He has accomplished through our lives. We have just celebrated our fiftieth year together and have always found the

Lord faithful. We have "stood" on the Scripture and found it absolute.

Jesus has given me real peace, complete satisfaction and perfect joy in life. Now I want to share Jesus with you so you can have what I have.

I want to tell you exactly how to find Jesus and to make Him a part of your life like He is a part of ours.

1. Recognize your need. Confess your sins — that you have come short of God's standard of holiness. *"All have sinned and come short of the glory of God."* Romans 3:23

2. Repent of your sins and recognize that they are transgressions against God, because you have broken His laws. *"Against thee, thee only, have I sinned, and done this evil in Thy sight."* Psalms 51:4

3. Ask God to forgive your sins. Your sins cannot be eliminated for you have committed them. But they can be forgiven. *"In whom we have redemption through His blood, even the forgiveness of sins."* Colossians 1:14 Only God can forgive sins. But when He does forgive them, they are gone forever. *"As far as the east is from the west, so far hath He removed our transgressions from us."* Psalms 103:12

4. Now accept Jesus Christ as your personal Saviour. God is offering you salvation through His Son. It is a free gift. *"The wages of sin is death; but the gift of God is eternal life through Jesus Christ our Lord."* Romans 6:23

Invite Him to come into your heart and receive Him as He comes. *"As many as received Him, to them gave He power to become the sons of God, even to them that believe on His name."* John 1:12

Now thank Him that He has come in and turn your life over to His guidance and strength. Always remember Jesus loves you and said in His Word, *"I am the resurrection and the life: he that believeth in Me, though he were dead, yet shall he live. And whosoever liveth and believeth in Me shall never die."* John 11:25-26

Gunda and Charles Robertson, 1985